The New Coach's Guide to Coaching Youth Soccer

Also by Robert L. Koger

101 Great Youth Soccer Drills

The New Coach's Guide to Coaching Youth Soccer

A Complete Reference to Coaching
Young Players Ages 4 through 8

ROBERT L. KOGER

Skyhorse Publishing

Skyhorse Publishing books may be purchased in bulk at special discounts for sales promotion, corporate gifts, fund-raising, or educational purposes. Special editions can also be created to specifications. For details, contact the Special Sales Department, Skyhorse Publishing, 307 West 36th Street, 11th Floor, New York, NY 10018 or info@skyhorsepublishing.com.

Skyhorse® and Skyhorse Publishing® are registered trademarks of Skyhorse Publishing, Inc.®, a Delaware corporation.

Visit our website at www.skyhorsepublishing.com.

10 9 8 7 6 5 4 3 2 1

Library of Congress Cataloging-in-Publication Data
Koger, Robert L.
The new coach's guide to coaching youth soccer : a complete reference to coaching young players ages 4 through 8 / Robert L. Koger.
p. cm.
Includes bibliographical references and index.
ISBN-13: 978-1-60239-031-7 (hardcover : alk. paper)
ISBN-10: 1-60239-031-2 (harcover : alk. paper)
1. Soccer for children—Coaching. I. Title.
GV943.8.K64 2007
796.334083—dc22
2007010870

Cover design by Adam Bozarth
Cover photo credit Ana Abejon

Print ISBN: 978-1-63220-688-6
Ebook ISBN: 978-1-63220-945-0

Printed in China

Contents

Preface

Chances are you went to sign up your child to play soccer and walked away as a coach. Well, let me say congratulations. Are you a little scared? Are you worried that you don't know what to do? Don't be afraid: you have just signed up to have a lot of fun. It may not seem like it now, but you have already taken the first big step. You have taken the initiative to learn more about the game of soccer. This book is written for you.

The New Coach's Guide to Coaching Youth Soccer is designed for new parent coaches with little or no experience in coaching or in soccer and with players 4 to 8 years of age in their charge. You may be using this book for five years or more, so sit back, get comfortable, and take everything one step at a time.

All coaches want their players to be the very best they can. To the player, soccer is just a fun game. Coaches and parents may be looking ahead to high school or even college. Scholarships are possible if the players learn properly. Having this book means that you have taken an initial giant step in learning the game of soccer and letting your players reach their maximum potential.

Your knowledge of the game will help in improving your team's skills and knowledge. This will aid their development in the game. Remember that soccer is more than just another activity. Playing soccer is an opportunity for children to socialize and get physical exercise in a safe, structured environment—an opportunity for families to enjoy activities together and to provide critical support to children developing confidence and a sense of identity.

One of my favorite quotes, which I think aptly applies to new coaches of youth players, is by H. L. Mencken: "The best teacher, until one comes to adult pupils, is not the one who knows the most, but the one who is most capable of reducing knowledge to that simple compound of the obvious and the wonderful which slips into the infantile comprehension . . . The best teacher of children, in brief, is one who is essentially childlike."

The more fun you make the game for the children playing the game, and the more you make the game enjoyable for the whole family, the more successful you will be. Have fun and enjoy being a soccer coach.

The New Coach's Guide to Coaching Youth Soccer

1

Getting Started as a Soccer Coach

You have already taken two steps toward getting started as a coach. You have signed up to coach a team, and you have purchased a book to assist you in doing the job correctly. The information in this book is designed for those coaching players between the ages of 4 and 8. There is some information on older players used to demonstrate the progression of training and development for soccer players, but the focus is on the youngsters.

Depending on where you are located, the name of the soccer organization you are involved with may be termed an association, a league, or a club. In most cases they mean the same thing. You will have a governing organization with different age groups and teams making up that organization.

Now that you are part of the organization, here is the important information you need to get started.

COACHING ESSENTIALS

Information Packet

Every coach receives an information packet. This is given to you when you sign up to coach or at the first coaches meeting. The packets vary in content but usually have a team roster so you can list all of your players, their addresses, and their phone numbers. Game cards which are blank are usually included so you can fill them out to list the names and uniform numbers of your players.

The game card is turned into the referee prior to the start of the game. You will need one for each game your team plays. The packet also usually contains insurance forms, bylaws/rules, and often information about sponsors. Don't wait for the meeting to start getting ready. Go online or contact your age group commissioner for information.

Parents Meeting

It is advisable to conduct a meeting with the parents prior to the start of practices. This is very important to establish who you are and what the parents can expect from you, as well as what you expect from them. Look in the table of contents of this book and you will find a section in chapter 8 labeled "Parents Meeting." The meeting contents are scripted so you can read it or paraphrase it when talking to your team's parents.

Notebook

One key item that you will need as a coach is a notebook. A spiral notebook that is about half the size of a full notebook is ideal because it will easily fit into your soccer bag or on your clipboard. Also a mechanical pencil easily fits into the spiral binding. This book will be used to keep all of your important soccer information in one location.

Keep your notebook accessible. If you pass a soccer field and see a team practicing and they are using drills that look good, stop and write down a diagram and information about the drill. This will help you expand your knowledge and, eventually, become a better coach. Also, remember there are many very good coaches and referees who are knowledgeable about soccer. If you are having problems with a certain drill, skill, or even a parent, don't hesitate to call an official in the organization and then record the information you received in your book. My books contain over twenty-five years of information that I constantly referred to.

Use of Drills

Teaching the skills is the important first step, but refining these skills is a must. This is accomplished by practicing the skills. Practice is achieved with a progressive set of skill development steps called soccer drills.

Drills are a necessity for every soccer player, as they provide the key to progressing from an understanding of the basics of a skill to becoming an advanced player with great soccer skills. As you coach your team, drills must be an essential part of every practice.

VALUABLE SOURCES OF INFORMATION

Internet

If you have access to a computer and the Internet, go online and see if your soccer organization has a Web site. Most do because it makes it easier to disseminate the much needed information. If you do not know the name of the Web site, just go to a popular search engine like Google or Yahoo and type in the organization's name, plus your city and your state. The reason for putting in your city and state is because there are thousands of soccer organizations and the name of yours may be the same as others.

Contacts

When you get onto the Web site, look for an area labeled contacts. These are sometimes under the heading of Board of Directors, Officials, or just Contacts. Look for two people who will be key contacts for you:

The first is the age group commissioner. This person will be identified as a commissioner or director and the title will be followed by U-6, U-8, etc. U-6 means 6 years of age and under. U-8 means 6-, 7-, and 8-year-olds. The determination of the exact ages for each grouping of players will be found in the organization's bylaws, which are sometimes called rules. Some organizations are very large, and as such they have pure age groups made up of 4-year-olds only, 5-year-olds only, and so on. Some also have boys age 4 and girls age 4 and the same on up. Write the name and the number of this person on the first page of your notebook. If it's provided on the Web site, you may also want to list his or her e-mail address. This will be the person who will be able to answer all of your questions pertaining to your team.

The second person you want to put into your notebook is the director of coaching development. This is the person who will set up training and licensing clinics for you and the other coaches. Training clinics are usually mandatory and are always very beneficial to new coaches.

Coaching Information

The next place to look on the Web site is under the title of "Coach Information," or something similar. Quite often this Web page will have information on upcoming clinics so you can see which dates are best for you before you contact the director of coaching. This page often also contains a printable copy of the bylaws or rules.

Bylaws/Rules

Make sure you print out a copy of the bylaws/rules and read them thoroughly. This document will provide the definition of the age groups, by birth date, as well as the number of players on the team, usually three or four players for U-6 and six or seven for U-8.

Since each organization can set its number of players per age bracket, it's essential to read the bylaws/rules. You will learn the ball size your team will use; the size of the field you will play on; when you can substitute; if you play with a goal-keeper; and everything else you need to know about the rules specific to age group.

Keep a copy of the bylaws/rules on your clipboard so you can refer to it when needed.

Practice

Call your age group director and find out which fields are available for your team to use for practice. Most organizations have areas that can be reserved. If they don't have any or they are all taken, contact the local elementary schools for permission to use their playground after school is closed for the day. Either way you will be able to get a field and not have to worry about its upkeep (mowing, etc.).

Also find out where the game fields are so you can drive to them and look them over to give yourself a better idea of field size. While you are at the field, write down the size of the opening of the goal and the distance from the corner of the field to the goal. You will need this information later for your practices.

Weather

Many organizations post the field conditions on their web sites to let you know if the practice and game fields are open for play. This will save you time trying to reach someone by phone or going to the field only to find out that it is not playable.

2

The Soccer Field

Knowing the name and layout of the field is a must for every soccer coach. Knowing the names of the field areas, and how each is used helps you to better understand the game of soccer. Your soccer players must also learn the field as they advance. Learning the field layout and using the terms as you talk to your team can help accomplish this. Using correct terminology and field structure will aid your team in their soccer development.

The entire soccer field is defined, although on many U-6 and U-8 fields some of the markings will not be used. The field will always be marked with a touchline, end/goal line, and center line. Other markings may be omitted as a cost-savings method.

The soccer field layout is rectangular and is the same design for all ages, but the dimensions vary depending upon location and age division. As the players get older, they play on larger fields. Fields are often hard to find and some are in areas that do not allow for the maximum field size. As a general rule, the younger players will use smaller fields.

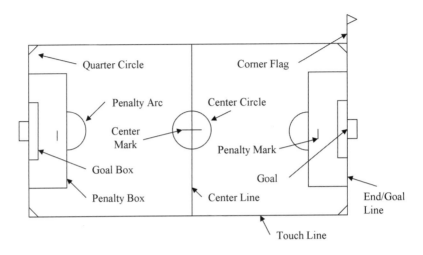

Figure 2.1. Soccer Field

Center Circle

Inside the center circle is where the game is started, with a kickoff. The defensive or opposing team is required to stay outside the circle until the ball is put into motion by the offensive team.

The offensive team puts the ball on the center mark, or spot, and rolls or kicks the ball to start the play. No defensive players can be in the center circle, but the offense can have as many as they want inside the circle. Usually only two offensive players enter the center circle.

Center Line

The center line divides the field into two halves. At the start of play from the center circle, each team is required to stay on their half until the ball is put into play.

Touchline

The touchline is the line running down the side of the field. In other sports this line is called the sideline. In soccer the line is called the touchline because this is the only place the field players are allowed to touch the ball with their hands. (Goalkeepers may touch the ball with their hands as long as they are inside their own penalty box.)

When the ball rolls out of the field of play by going over the touchline, the team that did not kick the ball out restarts the play by throwing the soccer ball back into the field of play. There is a required way to throw in the ball. If the throw-in is not done correctly, the referee stops the game and awards the ball to the opposing team for them to throw-in. The proper method for executing a throw-in is detailed in chapter 5.

End Line/Goal Line

The end line, which is sometimes called the goal line, is located at each end of the field and runs from corner to corner. This end line goes through the goal. The area of the end line inside the parameters of the goal is called the goal line. Like the touchline, when the ball goes over the end line, the ball is out of play and the game must be restarted.

A restart is accomplished by a kick from the goal box if the ball was kicked out of play by the offense, or by a corner kick if the ball was kicked out of play by the defense.

Quarter Circle

There is a quarter circle marking in each corner of the field. When the ball is kicked over the end line by the team that's defending the goal, the ball is put back into play by the offensive players by placing the ball inside the quarter circle and kicking or passing it out of the quarter circle. This is called a corner kick.

Goal Box

The goal box is the small box directly in front of the goal. When the ball is kicked out of play over the end line by the offensive team, the game is restarted by the defending team taking their "goal kick" from this box. The ball can be placed anywhere on the goal box line but is customarily placed in the front corner of the box on the side where the ball went out of bounds.

Penalty Box

The penalty box is the large box at each end that incorporates the goal box. Only in this area is the goalkeeper permitted to touch the ball with his or her hands. When a direct penalty, a major infraction of the rules, is committed inside the penalty box by the team defending the goal against a player on the team trying to score, the ball is placed on the penalty mark by the referee.

At this time the offensive team that was fouled selects a player to kick the ball toward the goal. The only other player that is allowed inside the penalty box at this time is the defending team's goalkeeper. The goalkeeper must stand on the end line, inside the goal, and is not permitted to move until the offensive player kicks the ball.

Once the offensive player kicks the ball, both teams may enter the penalty area. If the goalkeeper blocks the kick or the ball bounces off of the goal posts, then play resumes. If the ball is kicked into the goal then the offensive team scores, the ball is placed inside the center circle, and play is restarted. If the ball misses the goal and goes out of the field of play, then the game is restarted by a goal kick.

If a foul resulting in a direct kick is committed inside the penalty box by the offense, the defensive team takes the kick. This kick is like any other direct kick. No special restart is required.

Penalty Arc

An arc is located on the outside of the penalty box, in the center of the field. The purpose of the penalty arc is to ensure that all players are at least ten yards away from the ball during a penalty kick. This distance is a requirement for all penalty kicks. All opposing team members must stay at least ten yards away from the ball to allow the team playing the ball to start the play. When there is a penalty kick on the penalty mark, the arc line marks the distance ten yards away.

Penalty Spot or Mark

The penalty mark is where the ball is placed, by the referee, to be kicked by the offensive player when there has been a major foul committed by the defending team, inside the penalty box. On a regulation-sized field, the penalty mark is located twelve feet from the center of the goal, but on youth fields the distance is often shorter.

Corner Flag

A flag on a flexible pole is placed inside each of the quarter circles to mark the corner of the field. This flag enables the players on the field to be able to see the far corners of the field. The players have a hard time seeing the boundaries of the field while they are playing. The flags help them see the extreme areas of the field.

Center Spot

The center spot is marked by a circle, X, or short line in the middle of the center circle. This is where the ball is placed for kickoffs to start or restart play.

Goal

A goal is placed at each end of the soccer field. The goal is physically located in the center of the field, with the front edge of the goal placed on the end line. The net and goal frames are off the field. The goal has two goal posts and a cross bar as well as a net to cover the back of the goal and stop the ball when the ball is kicked into it.

The goal is placed directly on the end line and the end line is even with both goal posts. For a goal to be scored, the ball must travel completely across the end line and be within the borders of the goal. When a ball is stopped on the line, inside the goal, no goal is scored.

3

Understanding the Game

PLAYER POSITIONS DEFINED

There are established playing positions on the soccer field. These positions are called by different names to describe where the player is located or what the player does on the field. In many of the age groups the numbers of these players are reduced from the full eleven-player team.

Play with reduced teams can be called small-sided games, micro-soccer, or small-sided teams. The purpose is to allow the younger players to fully participate. With fewer players and a smaller field, each player gets more opportunities to have actual contact with the ball and to get more involved in the game.

This section covers the location of these players independent of the number of players on the field. Not all age groups will use all positions, as noted in chapter 17.

At this point we are going to go with the four main positions and names: forward, halfback, fullback, and goalkeeper. Figure 3.1 shows the player's positions relative to the other positions; the diagram does not show formation.

Remember, no matter what the position, when the team is on offense, all players play offense, when on defense, all players play defense. No one is strictly offense or defense. To play as a team, all players must play as one. This concept is very important and you must emphasize it to your team.

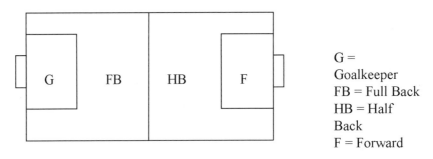

G = Goalkeeper
FB = Full Back
HB = Half Back
F = Forward

Figure 3.1. Positions

Goalkeeper

The primary job of the goalkeeper, keeper, or goalie is to stop the opposing team's players from scoring. The goalkeeper is the only player who can use his or her hands while on the field of play. Other team players can throw the ball into the field of play from outside the touchline.

The goalkeeper can touch the ball anywhere inside the penalty area. Outside of the penalty area, the goalie must play like all other players by using his or her feet only. The goalie wears a uniform shirt different in color than those worn by both teams' field players. This is to distinguish the goalie from the other players. When the goalkeeper catches the ball play stops until the ball is entered back into play by the goalie, who either throws or kicks the ball either to a teammate or just out into the field of play.

The goalkeeper directs the defense. With younger players, do not keep just one player in the goal all of the time. Field skills will not develop if the same player is always playing goalie. Rotation of players in and out of the goal is a must. The primary characteristics of a goalie are self-confidence, self-sufficiency, and individualism.

Fullback

The fullbacks are the closest players to the goal and their job is to be the last line of defense. They are the players that work with the goalkeeper to ensure the opposing team does not score. The fullbacks also start the ball on offense and normally take the goal kicks. The primary characteristic of a fullback is strength—being a strong team player who can bond with the other fullbacks and is very possessive and fully believes no one can get past him or her to score.

Halfback

The halfback's (or midfielder's) position is between the fullbacks and the forwards. They are the transition team that moves the ball from the offense to the defense and, conversely, from the defense to the offense. They also fight the midfield battle.

Most games are won or lost in the midfield. When a fullback has the ball and moves the ball up the field, the corresponding halfback drops back to cover the fullback position for the fullback who moved forward.

When the team moves into offense, the halfbacks either back up the forwards or move into the forward position. A primary characteristic of a halfback is to be a jack-of-all-trades. Halfbacks are players who can shift from defense to offense in a split second. They do not see themselves as belonging to the fullbacks or forwards, yet they play both roles. They are usually energetic and possess good overall soccer skills.

Forward

The forwards are at the opposite end of the field from their goal-keeper and closest to the opposing team's goal. Their job is to score or, failing that, to regain possession of the ball after making an attempt on goal. A primary characteristic of a forward is self-confidence. A forward is a self-sufficient person, with good speed and good ball-handling capabilities.

NOTE: One way many coaches initially pick players is by personality. Most parents want their child to play forward, which is considered the glory position. If the coach asked the parents what position they wanted their child to play, the result would be a team of only forwards. Not every player is best suited to play forward, however.

As a coach, you will be the one to place the players into positions. Most times the position you select will be a perfect placement for the player. However, if you think a player would be better in another position, move him or her. Remember, you have the final say in where the members of your team play. Most coaches will tell the parents why they have placed their children in the positions they are playing. Communication is a must for all coaches.

4

Rules of the Game

The best way to learn the complete rules of soccer is to get a book on the current Fédération Internationale de Football Association, or FIFA, Laws of the Game. Most soccer organizations have bylaws/rules on their Web page or give a copy to all of the coaches. These bylaws/rules cover how the FIFA rules have been modified to allow small-sided play. Many organizations also provide a full book on the rules. Ask your age group commissioner about these items.

The rules in this section are general to give you an overall concept of the simplicity and structure of the rules governing soccer.

BASIC RULES

Start of Play

Normally the team designated as the home team on the playing schedule gets to kick off and start the play of the game. Some organizations flip a coin to determine who kicks off first. During a kickoff, the ball must move forward and has to be touched by another player before it can be touched again by the person who kicked off.

The kicking team must be behind the person kicking off and all must be on that half of the field. The opposing team must all be in the opposite half and outside the center circle to allow the ball to be started in motion by the kicking team.

After a goal is scored, the ball is again placed in the center circle on the center spot and is kicked off by the team that did not score. Each quarter or half is started with a kickoff, with the teams alternating.

If play is stopped, the game is restarted by a drop ball, which means the ball is dropped by the referee between two opposing players and must touch the ground before being kicked. If the ball is kicked prior to touching the ground, the referee will re-drop the ball.

Ball Size

U-6 uses a size-3 ball. U-8 and U-10 use a size-4 ball. U-12 sometimes uses a size-4 ball. Players in an age group of U-14 or above use a regulation size-5 ball.

Number of Players

U-6 uses three or four players and does not use a goalkeeper. U-8 normally uses six or seven players with one being the goalkeeper. U-10 through U-12 normally use eight to ten players, and U-14 and above use a full eleven players. Again, check your organization's bylaws/rules to see the specific number your organization uses.

Game Duration

The games for U-6 and U-8 are generally divided into quarters of play so it is easier for the coach to ensure all players play an equal amount of time. Equal distribution of playing time is mandatory for younger age group players. The running time for U-6 and U-8 is up to ten-minute quarters with a two-minute break between quarters and five minutes at half time.

Games consisting of players in the U-10 and above age group use the standard two half periods. Each half will vary in length depending upon the age of the players. The halves normally vary from 20 minutes to standard 45 minute halves.

Ball Out of Play

The ball is out of play when it completely crosses over the touch-line or end line. When the referee stops the game by blowing the whistle, the ball is also out of play.

If the ball rolls onto one of the boundary lines of the field but does not go completely over the line, it is still in play. The ball is also in play if it bounces off the goal post, another player, a referee, or any other object and stays in the field of play.

Scoring

A goal is scored when the entire ball has traveled completely beyond the goal line and is inside the top and side posts of the goal. Use of hands or arms to propel the ball into the goal is a foul and goals scored in that manner will not count.

Substitutions

In youth soccer, player substitutions are unlimited in number but can only be made during designated times in the game. A player substitution must also be approved by the referee. The player entering the game must stand off the field of play and one to two yards back from where the center line intersects the touch line on your side of the field. Most U-6 teams are allowed to substitute a player at any time. All other age groups must wait for the following times:

- Prior to a throw-in by your team.
- Prior to a throw-in by the opposing team, if they are substituting.
- Prior to any goal kick by either team.
- After any goal scored by either team.
- After an injury to either team if the referee stops play.
- When a player is yellow-carded, which is an official warning for committing a foul that can cause harm to a player or players, you can substitute for that player. The opposing team can also substitute one player.

Player Clothing Requirements

Players cannot wear anything that is considered dangerous to themselves or other players on the field. The referee has the final authority on what can and cannot be worn. Normal items that cannot be worn are earrings, bracelets, rings, and glasses without a safety strap.

All players must wear athletic shoes or approved soccer shoes. Shin guards are required for all players in youth soccer. These shin guards are mandatory in practice and in games. Any player failing to wear shin guards will not be allowed to play or practice.

FOULS

Minor Fouls (Indirect Kick)

An indirect kick is the result of a foul being committed that was an infraction of the rules but not considered extremely dangerous. The game is stopped when the referee calls the foul, and the ball is placed on the ground at the spot of the infraction. The team that was fouled takes the kick and the ball must go on an indirect route to the goal—in other words, the soccer ball must be touched by another player besides the one who originally kicked it. If the ball goes directly into the goal, this will not count as a goal scored. If it touches another player from either team prior to going into the goal, then it will count as a goal scored.

The ball is placed on the ground and the players from the opposing team must be a designated distance away from the ball at the time of the kick. The referee gives a hand signal by holding his arm straight up in the air. The most common minor fouls are:

Obstruction
This is called when a player is intentionally holding or blocking another player.

Dangerous play
This can be any action that is deemed dangerous to other players on the field, but does not result in any harm.

Goalkeeper interference
This is called when an opposing player is blocking the goalkeeper, hits or runs into the goalkeeper, or does anything else that stops the goalkeeper from playing and releasing the ball.

Charging
This is when a person charges another when they are not near the ball. It can be pushing, bumping, hitting, or any other inappropriate action.

Leaving or entering the field
No player or coach can enter and no player can leave the field while the game is in play. A player must be completely off the field prior to another player entering the field. No player may enter or leave the field without referee permission. This also applies to the coach. You must have permission to enter the field,

even if you have a player hurt. Most referees will motion the coach onto the field. If they do not, just yell "permission to enter," and wait for the reply.

Major Fouls (Direct Kick)

A direct kick is not used for U-6 teams and most U-8 teams. A major foul is the result of a dangerous play committed by a player. This foul results in the stoppage of play and the direct kick is awarded to the team that was fouled. This means the ball can be kicked directly into the goal and count as a goal scored without first being touched by another player.

To make the direct kick, the ball is placed on the ground at the spot of the infraction, and the players from the opposing team must remain ten yards away from the ball at time of the kick. The referee signals with an arm straight out and pointed directly at the point of infraction.

The referee must explain all infractions to the offending player, not to the coach or to the spectators. No caution or ejections shall be issued to the player except by an independent neutral referee.

The following are infractions or fouls that result in direct kicks:

Tripping
This is a deliberate attempt by a player to trip an opponent, usually with one's feet.

Handling the ball
This is intentional touching of the ball with your hands while on the field of play. (The exception is the goalkeeper, while he or she is in the penalty area.)

Jumping at another player
This involves any jump that is dangerous and could cause injury to another player.

Charging from behind
This is the act of running into or hitting a player from behind or from the player's blind side.

Dangerous charge
This is any hit on a player that is dangerous and could seriously hurt him or her.

Pushing
This is usually a result of players trying to get to the ball while they have their hands out. Pushing is anything that results in the opposing player being shoved and thrown off balance.

Holding
This can be called by holding the person or the uniform. A hold is called if the other player cannot advance due to the hold.

Striking
This is just another word for hitting a player.

Kicking or attempting to kick another player
Players are going to be kicked in a game. The action may or may not be called. Many younger players follow the ball rather than play a set formation and end up in a group where everyone is kicking. When the ball shoots out there may be two or more players lying on the ground because they were kicked. This is not normally called, but can be.

WARNING AND EJECTION CARDS

When a grave foul, major or minor, has been committed, the referee can issue a card to the player. That means the referee will hold up a colored card to indicate the type of penalty.

This is held in plain view so the player and the coach can see the card.

The yellow card is a warning card, a caution, to inform the player he or she has committed a serious infraction. If the player repeats the infraction, or receives multiple yellow cards, that player can be ejected from the game.

Yellow cards are shown to players for:
- Dangerous play
- Improper conduct
- Persistent fouls
- Dissent

The red card is an ejection card. When this card is displayed the player must leave the field and cannot be replaced by another player. The team continues to play short that player.

Red cards are shown to players for:
- Persistent fouls after caution
- Violent play
- Abusive language

Check your league rules or with the director of referees, as some leagues allow only so many lost points due to cards, and then disciplinary actions are taken against the team. Some leagues make the person getting the red card sit out the next game. The team can play with a full team, but the person that received the red card in the previous game cannot play the following game. Read the local bylaws/rules that apply to your organization, and if you still have questions, contact the director of referees or your age group commissioner.

CHANGING GOALKEEPER

You are allowed to switch the goalkeeper on a penalty kick. If your goalie is hurt on a play, or if your team has another goalie that is good at blocking penalty kicks, this player can be sent in on a goalkeeper change prior to the kick. However, after the players are changed, your team must wait until you have an authorized substitution time before changing back to the original goalkeeper.

ADVANTAGE RULE

The advantage clause applies to a rule that says: if an infraction occurs, but would penalize the team with the ball, the referee can direct the players to continue to play as if no infraction occurred.

When a penalty occurs but the same team keeps the ball, and maintains the advantage, the penalty is not called and as a result the foul does not punish the team that has been fouled.

If advantage is called by the referee, the call cannot be taken away. Sometimes the advantage call is made and then the team loses the ball. Once the call is made the call is final.

OFFSIDE RULE

The offside rule does not apply in U-6 games and is not used in most U-8 games either.

The offside call is probably the most disliked and debated call in soccer. Simply put, the player is deemed to be offside if the player is an offensive player, does not have the ball, and has fewer than two opposing players between him- or herself and the opponent's goal line. This stops a team from placing a player directly in front of the goal and enables the defense to move away from the goal, also making the offensive team move away.

Another offside condition exists if the player is nearer the opponent's goal line than the ball, and the ball is played through to him. As soon as the ball is kicked, the offensive player can move beyond the last defender. Since the referee will be positioned near the ball, the side judges often make these calls, because they have a better vantage point.

The determination of whether the player was on or offside is often a judgment call. Sometimes, faster players are called offside when they were not. Offside is easier to explain by describing what is not offside:

The player is in his or her own half
If your players are in their own half when the ball is kicked, the half that has your goalkeeper, they cannot be offside.

There are at least two defenders between player and goal
Anytime there is more than one defender between the offensive player and the goal, this player cannot be offside. This is normally the goalkeeper and one fullback. The team on defense should move their players toward the centerline as the ball goes down the field. This pulls the offense away from your team's goal and gives the defense time to get the ball in case the ball is kicked over their heads.

Throw-in, corner kick, goal kick, and drop ball
Since these are restarts, the offside rule does not apply on the initial play. However, as soon as the ball is touched by another player, the offside rule is back in effect.

5

Start and Restart Actions

Throughout the game, there will be times when play is started and stopped. The game will start with a kickoff and will start again after the quarters and after halftime. Besides the scheduled starts, other times include when the ball goes out of play, a goal is scored, or the game is stopped by the referee. When these things happen the game is restarted through different means. This chapter covers the start and restart actions.

Kickoff

The kickoff is used to start play for the first and second half as well as to start the quarters. The kickoff is also used as a restart after a goal is scored. The kickoff is always from the center circle. After a score, the team that did not score is given the ball and they kickoff. The defensive (opposing) team is required to stay outside the circle until the ball is put into motion by the offensive team (the team that has the ball). The offensive team puts the ball on the center mark and rolls or kicks the ball to start the play.

Drop Ball

During a drop ball, two players, one from each team, face each other and the ball is dropped straight down between the two players. When the ball touches the ground, the players can kick it. A drop ball is used when the ball goes off the field after being touched simultaneously by both players, or when the game is stopped and neither team has advantage or control of the ball. It's a way to restart the game without giving advantage to either team.

Throw-In

When the soccer ball leaves the field of play by going over the touchline, in the air, or on the ground, the opposing team will throw the ball back onto the field to re-start the game. The opposing team is the team that did not knock the ball out of play.

A proper throw-in requires the ball to be held with both hands over the head, a part of both feet on the ground, and the player facing the field of play. The throw must be made from behind the head, moving over the top of the head in a continuous motion. Both hands must be used equally so the ball spins forward and does not spin to the right or to the left. Neither foot can leave the ground until the ball has left the player's hands.

For the U-6 and U-8 teams, additional throw-ins are allowed if the first throw was incorrect. The referee will explain to the player what he or she did wrong, and then the player will get another chance to do it correctly. Above U-8 players only have one chance. If the throw is incorrect, the ball will be given to the opposing team to throw-in.

Like the kickoff, the ball must be touched by another player before the person throwing the ball can touch it again.

Goal Kick

A goal kick is used to put the ball back into play when the entire ball has rolled out of play over the end/goal line and was last touched by the attacking team—that is, the team trying to score a goal. To restart the play the team that did not kick the ball out of play places the ball on the ground inside the boundary of their own goal box and kicks it out into the field. If the ball does not go outside the penalty area before it is touched for the second time, the referee will stop play and the ball will be kicked again.

All members of the opposing team must remain outside of the penalty area and cannot touch the ball until the ball has cleared the penalty box. For U-6 and U-8 teams, the ball is normally placed up to three feet from the goal, and the referee will keep the players back from the ball to allow the ball to clear the direct goal area.

Corner Kick

When the ball is kicked out of play over the end/goal line and was last kicked by the team defending the goal, a corner kick is awarded to the opposing, or attacking team. The ball is taken to the nearest corner quarter circle and placed inside that quarter circle. An offensive team member will kick the ball out of the quarter circle to restart play. The ball must be touched by another player before it can again be touched by the original kicker.

Opposing team members must stay a designated distance from the ball allowing the player to kick the ball out into the field of play.

Indirect Kick

An indirect kick is the result of a penalty that is in the "minor foul" category. That means there was a foul committed, but it was not a dangerous act. When the referee calls the foul, play stops, the ball is placed on the mark of the foul, and the game is restarted with the kick.

An indirect kick means the ball must go on an indirect route to the goal. In other words, it must be touched by another player after it is originally kicked. If the ball goes directly into the goal, it will not count as a goal. If it touches another player from either team prior to going into the goal, then it will count as a goal.

To restart play, the ball is placed on the ground and the opposing team players must be at a designated distance away from the ball at time of the kick.

Direct Kick

A direct kick is not used in U-6 play. The direct kick is the result of a major penalty or foul which is considered dangerous. When the referee calls the foul, play stops, the ball is placed on the mark of the foul, and the game is restarted with the kick.

A direct kick means the ball can be kicked directly into the goal, and count as a goal, without being touched by another player. The ball is placed on the ground and the other players from the opposing team must be at a designated distance away from the ball at time of the kick.

Penalty Kick

A penalty kick falls in the category of a direct kick and as such is not used in U-6 play. Check with your organizational bylaws to see if it is used in U-8 play. A penalty kick is the result of a major foul by the defense that happens within their penalty area.

The ball is placed on a designated spot directly in front of the goal. The location is about halfway between the goal and the penalty box line.

One player from the team that was fouled is picked to kick the ball. The goalkeeper must stand on the end line, between the goal posts, and cannot move until the ball is kicked. All other players from both teams must stay outside the penalty box until the kick has taken place. If the ball hits the goal posts or is blocked by the goalie, the ball is back into play. If it goes outside the goal area and travels off the field, it is restarted by a goal kick. If the ball goes into the goal, it counts as a score and the game is restarted by a kickoff.

RULES FOR THE START AND RESTART OF PLAY

Most leagues have modified the start and restart rules for the younger players. The information provided here is the most common. Direct kicks and penalty kicks are not normally used in U-6 and U-8 play.

Start/Restart	Score	A Designated Distance to Allow Team to Place Ball in Play
Kickoff	No	Yes*
Throw-In	No	No (U-6 & U-8 will be given multiple chances to throw-in the ball properly)
Goal Kick	No	Yes*
Corner Kick	Yes	Yes*
Direct Kick	Yes	Yes (Not normally used for U-6 and U-8)*
Indirect Kick	No	Yes*
Drop Ball	Yes	No
Penalty Kick	Yes	Yes. Outside the penalty box. (Not normally used for U-6 & U-8)*

*Most leagues use 3 to 8 yards for U-6 and U-8 teams

6

Coach, Player, and Parent Equipment

This chapter covers the equipment that is needed for the coach, player, and parent. The list of items in this chapter may seem overwhelming at first, but many of the items are inexpensive and many are items you may already have.

All of the items in this chapter are common soccer equipment and are easy to find. Many discount stores, used sporting goods stores, and soccer stores sell these items, often in a package deal.

COACH EQUIPMENT
The following items are equipment that's recommended for you to be able to properly conduct practices and games:

Large Waterproof Equipment Bag
This is required for storage of your team's equipment—the extra soccer balls, cones, etc., in one place for easy access. If you can't find a waterproof bag, put a large trash bag inside your equipment bag. This can be used to cover your bag in case of rain.

Cones

The use of cones, plastic and of any color, is critical when coaching. They will be used in just about every drill. Having the cones also enables you to establish the limits or design of the drill. Cones can be purchased at practically any sporting goods store and are often sold in discount stores.

The most common color for the cones is safety orange. Be sure to mark your cones using a permanent marker to identify whose they are, in case they are left on the field after practice by mistake. All you need to mark on the cones is your name and phone number. Don't put on your address.

Whistle

A whistle is a necessity. The whistle saves your voice and also enables the players to get use to responding to the whistle on the field. You can use the whistle to start and stop play, drills, or anything else you do on the field. Whistles can be purchased that hang around your neck or around your wrist. Use the one that is easiest for you.

Water Jug

Be sure to tell each player to bring water to every practice and game. Some players will forget their water bottle, so having a team water jug is important. The players will be constantly moving during practice and games and can easily get dehydrated.

An expensive and very large water container is not necessary. Usually a three to five gallon container is adequate. This can be filled at home and ice cubes can be added, if wanted. Also, keeping the water container small will enable you to carry it more easily.

Purchasing small, inexpensive, disposable cups are also a good idea. The cups will end up on the ground and you will have to constantly remind the players to pick them up.

Chalkboard/Clipboard

A chalkboard or clipboard with a diagram of the field is a necessity. Small children, and most adults, cannot visualize what you want unless they see what you want in relation to the field. I have seen coaches drawing with a stick in the dirt, and the players reacted to the instruction as though it were just a drawing in dirt.

I purchased a small chalkboard and used a permanent white marker to draw the field on the black background. I then used erasable chalk to draw plays or explain positions. I didn't use an eraser; I just grabbed an old sock and used that sock to erase the board. I did not like using a clipboard with a picture of the field on one side because the clipboard was always covered with papers and the pen was always dry when I needed to draw.

A clipboard is great to keep your roster and other paperwork handy, but constantly removing papers to get to the diagram of the field is not good. On your clipboard, be sure to use a rubber band around the bottom to prevent your papers from flying up.

Practice Shirts or Vests

When you run offensive and defensive drills, having different color shirts/vests for the players is a real asset. However, you do not have to go out and buy shirts or vests.

An easy way is to have each player bring an old shirt to practice that can be given to you. Have them bring a shirt that is white. Even if there is a picture on the shirt, it's okay. Take the shirts home and dye half of them a bright, but light color like yellow, light blue, pink, or any color you want. Leave the other half white. You now have practice shirts. You keep the shirts in your equipment bag so they don't get lost. This will require you to wash them every so often. For more on the shirt donation, see chapter 8, which covers the parents meeting.

Rubber Bands/Hair Clips

If you have girls or boys with long hair, carrying extra rubber bands or head bands is a great idea. Your players will show up with their hair untied sometimes. Give them a rubber band or head band to keep their hair out of their eyes.

Stopwatch

A stopwatch is nice but not a necessity. It is used so you can accurately know the time that has elapsed in the game. Most organizations require that all games for young players are split into quarters. If your organization uses the half system, using a stopwatch will let you know when half of the half, or a quarter of play, has elapsed and when it is time to put in additional players.

Small-Side Goal

You may also want to purchase what is commonly referred to as a small-side goal. This is a miniature goal that may be rectangular or half-moon shaped. The goal is usually around three to four feet wide and two to three feet high. Since the goal comes with a net, you and the players won't have to chase the ball after it goes into the goal. The goal is also very easy to store.

First Aid Kit

This item is a necessity to have. Keep a first aid kit in your equipment bag so it is handy. Your players will get cuts, scrapes, and bloody noses. If you do not have any medical training, check the local community for classes about first aid.

Extra Band-Aids are a must. You will go through them very fast. If you have a player that has a bad cut or scratch, you can also use a feminine napkin and adhesive tape. The napkin is padded and will absorb blood. Older players will not use these, but they are great for the younger players. Cartoon character band-aids are a favorite of the younger players and can go a long way toward stopping the inevitable crying that occurs when little ones get a cut or scrape.

Also keep some slip-on rubber medical gloves in your medical kit for when a player is bleeding. These can be purchased at most discount hardware stores.

Ziplock Bags

Carry some ziplock bags in your equipment bag. They are great for holding ice in case a player gets hurt. If you have the water container, you can reach in and grab the ice and fill the bag. Also, many parents bring ice chests to games.

The bags can also hold jewelry and other items the players hand to you to keep for them during practice or games.

Shoes

Comfortable shoes are a necessity. You will be on your feet the entire practice with your team, and will be running, standing, stopping, etc.

Although good coaches do not play with the team, they demonstrate and then let the team do the actual activity. Shoes that have a cloth top are not recommended since you may be kicking and do need the upper shoe support. If you practice in an area that has hard ground and thin grass, soccer shoes with high cleats will also cause your feet to hurt. A good athletic shoe or a general-purpose soccer shoe that has multiple low cleats is best.

Shorts

Most coaches wear shorts when they practice with their team, but you need to wear whatever you are comfortable wearing. Shorts are cooler and if you get soccer-style shorts, they allow freedom of movement. Many come with a back pocket to hold your items.

Shirt

For practice with your team, a comfortable T-shirt that allows airflow, is light in weight and color, and fits loosely is best.

For games, coaches differ in what they wear. Some like to wear a jersey that matches their team's colors. Some even have their name or "coach" put on the shirt. Some wear a pull over shirt that is the same color as the team's jerseys. This can continue to be worn for other events, even if your team changes its jersey color the next season. Finally, some coaches wear whatever happens to be handy in the closet. Again, the key is to be comfortable.

Pants and Hat

During games you will be standing or sitting for the duration. You will not be moving around very much. Wearing long pants and a hat will decrease your chance of getting sunburned. Protect yourself.

Ball Bag

As you start accumulating your own collection of soccer balls, a bag to carry them in will be necessary. Net ball bags are inexpensive and can be bought at most sports and discount stores. Having the soccer balls in the bag will enable you to carry them easily, and keep them in one place.

Cold Weather Clothing

Most areas have at least two soccer seasons each year. One is in the spring and the other in the fall. Some areas go year round. As a result, you will be going to practices and games during cold or inclement weather. Dress appropriately. Soccer is played in shorts and shirts, although some leagues allow the younger players to wear long sleeve shirts and even long pants under their uniforms.

Your team may play in the rain, if there is no lightning, and in the snow, sleet, etc. Make sure you and your players dress warmly. When the players are not on the field playing, they need to be in sweats or warm-up clothing. Blankets are great for the players and their parents. Standing on the side of the field with a very cold player is not an enjoyable experience. Warm players are better players, and warm parents are happy parents.

Cell Phone

Having a cell phone or access to one is always a good idea. You will have the phone for emergencies, and occasionally parents will be late to pick up their player. Having access to a phone will save you a lot of time. If you don't have one, check with the parents. Normally a few parents will always stay and watch the practices. See if you can use theirs, in case of an emergency.

PLAYER EQUIPMENT

Ball

The ball size for under age U-6 and U-8 is size 3. You have an option: you can have your players bring their own ball to every practice or have the players bring a ball that you then keep in a bag so it is always available for practice. Many children have more than one soccer ball so they won't be without a ball at home. Make sure each ball is marked, using a permanent marker or pen, with the player's name and phone number.

Look on the ball for the exact pressure requirement and then air the ball to that amount. The weight of the ball changes with the size. Size 3 is approximately nine ounces, size 4 is approximately twelve ounces, and size 5 is approximately fifteen ounces. However, air the ball until it is firm.

Footwear

Athletic shoes can be worn to play soccer. But the problem with this type of shoe is that it does not enable the player to stop, start, or move properly during the game. When buying soccer shoes, make sure they are soft for the foot and do not have a toe cleat. Athletic shoes with toe cleats are used for baseball and football. A toe cleat on soccer shoes can alter the kick or even hurt the player by stopping the forward motion of the foot during a kick, as it will dig into the ground.

> *NOTE:* Most children will outgrow their soccer shoes before they wear them out. The parents can help themselves by donating outgrown shoes that no longer fit their child. You or the team manager can keep a box in the truck of one of your cars that shoes can be dropped in.
>
> If there is a pair of soccer shoes already in the box that fits another player, have them take them. If you work with older teams and younger teams you will be able to recycle the shoes and save many parents from having to buy new pairs. You will have to work with older teams or the player with the biggest feet will always be buying new shoes.

Shin Guards

This is a mandatory item for all practices and games. Shin guards come in different styles and makes. Make sure only approved shin guards are used. You can get a shin guard that inserts into the sock and is held in place by the sock. The most common type is the shin guard that has straps that go around the calf of the leg and attaches using Velcro. There is also the type that has a loop or stirrup at the bottom of the shin guard that goes under the foot and pulls on like a sock. Although there are other types, these three are the most common.

Regardless of which kind of shin guard the player gets, they must have a pair. Approved shin guards are mandatory to wear during all practices and games. Shin guards prevent serious injuries to the shins. Do not ever let your players practice or play without shin guards. The players will be checked for shin guards by the referee prior to all games. Players that do not have shin guards will not be allowed to play.

With younger players, you will often also see kneepads. This gives the player confidence while they are learning the game. They know that if they fall, they will not be hurt. It is alright to let them use kneepads. They will outgrow the need for them.

Shorts

Soccer is a game that is played in shorts. The shorts need to be loose fitting to allow the player to move without restrictions. Players can wear actual soccer shorts or any shorts that meet the requirements.

Soccer shorts come with either an elastic waist or tie strings. The elastic waist shorts are usually much better to get for the younger players. If your team is young and small, the bottom of the shorts may cover some of the sock and go almost to the top of the shoes. That's okay.

Shirts

Soccer is a game of running, and as a result, the shirts the players wear need to be able to allow air to flow through. Most T-shirts will work. Heavy cotton or other types of materials that inhibit airflow are not recommended.

Socks

Socks used for soccer are knee length so they can cover the shin guards and also protect the legs from cuts and scrapes. Tube socks are fine if they are the proper length; however, socks that have padded feet are the best. Remember, your players will be doing a lot of running. Protection and comfort for the feet is a must.

Soccer Uniform

The soccer uniform is comprised of a shirt, shorts, and socks. Your team will wear matching shirts with different numbers. The two numbers that are the most requested are numbers 9 and 10. Nine is the number worn by Mia Hamm of the United States Women's National Team. The team's best player commonly wears the number 10. This was the number worn by both Pelé and Diego Maradona, perhaps the two greatest male soccer players in the history of the game.

The goalkeeper usually wears the number 1. Numbers 2 and up are normally worn by the forwards, the halfbacks, and the fullbacks. The goalkeeper is required to wear a shirt that is a different color than all other players' shirts. This is to distinguish the player as the goalkeeper.

Shorts must also be matching for all of your players. If a member of your team shows up with different color shorts, check with the referee. They will normally be allowed to play.

The goalkeeper will often wear padded shorts for protection when contacting the ground.

Your team socks can be any color, but all player's socks must match. Quite a few of the coaches want a distinctive color of socks for their team: red, blue, black, striped, etc. The reason is that the players will see the feet and legs of their teammates first when they are in close play. The color of the socks enables them to easily recognize their own teammates.

Jewelry

Jewelry cannot be worn on the field or at practice. This includes necklaces, rings, ear rings, bracelets, hair barrettes, etc. Wearing jewelry can cause injury. Earrings can get ripped out of the ear, rings can scratch other players, and necklaces can choke or cut a player's neck.

If your players wear jewelry to a practice or game, have them remove the jewelry before playing. If you cannot get a ring off a finger, wrap adhesive tape around both the ring and the finger.

Equipment Bag

Each player needs a bag large enough to hold shoes, water, a soccer ball, and anything else he or she may need to carry. This keeps everything in one location. The bag keeps them from losing items and teaches them to put their stuff away.

Many of the players will want a bag the same color as their team uniform. An expensive bag is not advisable since team colors sometimes change every year.

Water Bottle/Jug

Most coaches take water to practice and games, but players need to bring their own water to every practice and game. Due to the running and the heat, it's very easy to get dehydrated while playing soccer. Having water available will provide the players with all the liquids they need.

There are many different types of liquid containers on the market. Some are insulated to keep the water cool, and some are just plastic bottles. Some parents freeze a bottle of water and then give that bottle to their player to take to practice. The ice will melt in the heat, but the water will be cold. They can pick any type they want, but make sure the parents mark the container with the player's name.

Rubber Bands/Headbands

If you have a girl or boy with long hair on your team, it is a great idea for them to carry extra rubber bands or headbands. Players may show up with their hair untied and hanging in their face. Have them grab a rubber band or headband out of their bag to get their hair out of their eyes.

PARENT EQUIPMENT

Many parents will come to you to ask questions about what to do in different situations. The following is information to enable you to advise them.

Video/Film Set-Up

Many parents like to film their child while he or she is playing the game. The best position for filming or using a video camera is at the top of the bleachers. From this view they are looking down on the field and can use the zoom to get very good pictures.

If the field does not have bleachers, a ladder can be used. The parent can bring a lightweight, sturdy ladder. Standing on the ladder gives them the height they need to see the field and get a good downward view without being blocked by the players or other parents standing on the edge of the field.

Cameras are usually best when you are close to the action. Parents cannot go on the field or be behind the goal during the game, but they can move up and down the touchline to get good shots of their child or the team as long as they stay out of the way of the coach and sideline referee.

Scrapbook

Making a scrapbook is a good family activity. For my children I had separate ones for sports, school, and other activities. A scrapbook is fun to put together and really fun to look back at when the child has grown. I used the type that had a plastic film that I just pulled back to place the information inside.

You can go from very simple to very elaborate. Many organizations or communities will have write-ups about the games, either in a soccer newsletter, local newspaper, or on their Web site. Clip these out or print them out and add them to the book. Parents can also write up a small description of how their child played, the score of the game, etc. These can be accompanied by pictures. Tell the parents to start as their child starts playing. That way they have a good record of their child's activities. All children like the attention.

7

Referee and Referee Signals

REFEREE

First of all, referees are human. They are not monsters out to ruin your day. Referees are there to direct the play and enforce the rules of the game of soccer. Referees are very good and work very hard to make the correct calls. However, there will be some calls that are made that may not be correct. Get over it.

With the younger players, referees are often high school soccer players or college players who get a small sum for every game they referee. These young referees should be respected by you, your team's parents, and your players. Be sure you model the expected behavior.

All referee calls are final. Even referees calling the World Cup games make mistakes. This is part of the game. Arguing with a referee or yelling at a referee over a call is not a good idea and can often be counter-productive. I have never met a referee who was vindictive and did not try their best to do a great job.

You may see different referee configurations. You will always have a field referee, the referee that is on the field during the game. This can be the job of one referee who moves with the players on the field, or you may have two referees who move diagonally on each half of the field.

If using the one field referee configuration, which is the official setup, there will be two line judges, which are actually assistant referees, who move up and down the touchline, each covering one-half of the field. They carry a flag and raise the flag to tell the field referee there has been an infraction of the rules. These individuals normally make the offside calls and call penalties that occur behind the referee's back.

Line judges are often older soccer players who are working for part-time money. They usually know the rules very well and do a great job. You may also be asked to get a volunteer parent to run the lines, meaning be the line judge. Some leagues use this as a money-saving method. In this situation, the home team normally provides the volunteers. Make sure your volunteers are briefed on what they need to do and can be fair and equitable to both teams. They should not be openly cheering for your team. They are there as an official.

> **NOTE:** Your team can make the referee an extra player. Just about all referees are consistent in their calls. In other words, tell your team to go with the flow. The worst thing you, as a coach, can do is to get mad at the way the referee is calling the game. Your team will see this and your actions will impact their play. Also, when players get mad they take their mind off the game.
>
> Players cannot concentrate if they are mad. Keep telling your team to "play on," because they will not change the referee's mind. A player that does not get mad at other players, or referees, plays very consistently, and that is a must in soccer.

Knowing the calls made on the field by the referee and assistant referees, or linemen, is a necessity if you are to fully understand what is happening on the field. Many times you, or the spectators, may be looking at another area of the field and miss the infraction. By knowing the referee signals you can understand what happened.

This chapter covers the most common signals used by the field referee and the line judges. There are more, but these are the most common you will see.

REFEREE SIGNALS

A caution or expulsion is denoted by the referee stopping the game, pulling out a card, and holding the card in the air above the head. This is done so the player that committed the infraction can see the card and the color, and the card can also be seen by the coach and spectators.

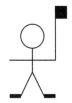

Figure 7.1.
Caution or Expulsion

A yellow-colored card is a caution or a warning to the person that committed the infraction of the rules. The yellow card notifies the person to stop that infraction.

A red-colored card is normally issued after a yellow card or caution has been given, but the player continues to commit the offense. A red card can be given with no prior warning if the action was unsportsmanlike or violent and could potentially harm other players.

A player can continue to play after issue of the yellow card. The coach can also elect to replace the player at that time. If a red card is issued, the player must exit the field and the team must play without that person. They will be playing a person short, compared to the other team.

Movement
Of
Hands

Figure 7.2. Play On, Advantage Rule

The advantage rule is applied when a team has possession of the ball and is fouled by the other team, but stopping play would remove advantage from the team with the ball. The referee will have both hands in front and will motion forward yelling "play on."

If after the "play on" call, the team loses the ball, the advantage rule cannot be reversed.

A direct kick is the result of a major foul. Direct means the ball can be kicked directly into the goal without touching any other

Figure 7.3. Direct Kick

player. The opposing team must give the player kicking the ball room to kick. This distance is normally 10 yards but is often shorter for younger players. If the opposing team is too close, the referee will move them back to the required distance.

The signal for a direct kick is an extended arm held straight away from the body (or extended and slightly elevated).

Figure 7.4. Indirect Kick

An indirect kick is the result of a minor foul. Indirect means the ball must take an indirect route to the goal. In other words, the ball must touch another player after the original kick before it can go into the goal. If it goes into the goal without touching another player, it does not count as a goal scored. A player from either team can touch the ball. If the ball is kicked directly toward the goal and is touched by the goalkeeper before going into the goal, it will count as a goal scored.

As with a direct kick, the opposing team must give the player kicking the ball room to kick it. This is normally 10 yards but is often shorter for younger players. If the opposing team is too close, the referee will move them back to the required distance.

The signal for an indirect kick is to extend the arm straight up from the body over the head.

If the ball has gone out of bounds by rolling over the touchline, play is restarted by a throw-in.

The referee will move to a point directly even with where the ball must be thrown from, and will extend the arm to indicate which team throws in the ball.

**Figure 7.5.
Direction of Throw-in**

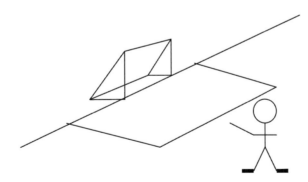

Figure 7.6. Goal Kick, Goal Scored, and Penalty Kick

The following three actions are similar in signal but are used at different times:

Goal kick

When the ball travels over the end line and was last touched by the offensive team, the defensive team restarts play by kicking the ball from their goal area.

The referee signal for this is to point at the corner of the goal box on the side of the field where the ball went out of bounds.

Goal scored

After a goal is scored the referee will point directly into the opening of the goal to indicate the goal is good and counts as a point for the offensive team.

Penalty kick

If a major infraction occurs inside the penalty area the referee will indicate a penalty kick by moving inside the penalty area and pointing directly at the penalty mark.

Figure 7.7. Corner Kick

When the ball goes over the end line and was last touched by the defensive team, the game is restarted by a corner kick.

The referee will point directly at the corner on the side of the field where the ball went out of bounds.

ASSISTANT REFEREE SIGNALS

The assistant referees are very important to the game and act as two more pairs of eyes for the referee. They are referred to by different names. Two of the names commonly used are linesman and flagger. In the younger team's games, the assistant referees are often volunteer parents from one or both of the teams that are playing on the field.

The assistant referee uses a flag with a short handle and stands outside the touchline. There is one assistant referee on each side of the field and that person moves from the end line to the centerline only. Each assistant referee controls a separate half of the field of play.

Remember, the referee will also be indicating the action.

Figure 7.8. Throw-in

A throw-in is signaled by the assistant referee pointing the flag in the direction in which the throw will be made. A team can throw anywhere on the field, but the flag will always point toward the goal the team is trying to score in.

In figure 7.9, the assistant referee points the flag directly toward the corner where the kick will take place. This indicates a corner kick.

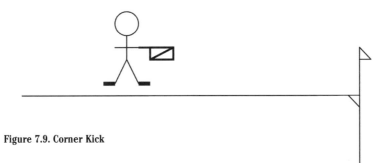

Figure 7.9. Corner Kick

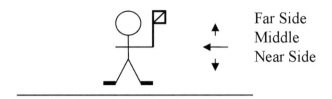

Far Side
Middle
Near Side

Figure 7.10. Offside

Offside is usually called by the assistant referee and the position of the flag tells the referee where the infraction took place. Holding the flag straight up in the air means the offside was on the far side of the field. Pointing straight out onto the field means the offside was in the middle of the field. Pointing straight down means the infraction was on the near side of the field.

This enables the referee to call the play without going over to the touchline and talking to the assistant referee.

Offsides is one of the most difficult calls to make, and assistant referees are prone to make mistakes from time to time when calling it.

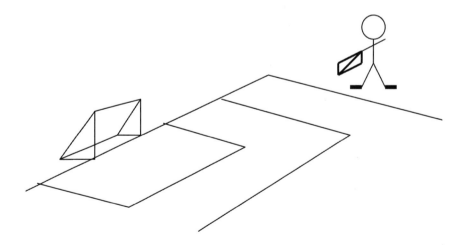

Figure 7.11. Goal Kick

To indicate a goal kick, the assistant referee stands directly out from the goal box and points the flag toward the corner of the goal box. The assistant referee will hold the flag until the kick has been taken.

When a team wants to make a substitution, they must have the approval of the referee. To indicate that the coach wants to make a substitution, the assistant referee holds the flag directly overhead and parallel to the ground. When the referee sees this they will either allow or deny a substitution at that time.

Figure 7.12. Substitution

When the ball has gone out of bounds, or out of play, the assistant referee will hold the flag straight up to indicate to the referee that the ball is out of play.

Figure 7.13. Ball Out of Play

When the assistant referee needs to get the attention of the referee, that person will raise the flag overhead and wave it from side to side. The popping action of the flag can be heard, and the referee will respond.

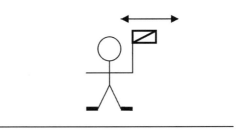

Figure 7.14. Getting the Referee's Attention

8

Starting the Season

PARENTS MEETING

Holding a parents meeting is one of the most important steps you will take as a new coach. More coaches quit every year due to problems with parents than any other reason. Many outstanding coaches refuse to coach because of parents who get out of control.

Establishing your goals for the team and your ground rules up front and then sticking to them is very important. This will save you many headaches and make your coaching experience fun and rewarding.

The parents meeting should be conducted prior to the first practice. This is a must for you and for the parents.

The following is a sample outline including sample language you can use that will enable you to establish and conduct a parents meeting. Using it will allow you to establish the parameters and guidelines necessary to have a fun and productive soccer season.

STEP ONE: ARRANGING THE MEETING

Call all of the parents. Set a time and place for your meeting. Let the parents know that the meeting will last approximately thirty to forty-five minutes. Since this is a meeting for the parents, you do not want the players to attend.

Some parents will still bring their children, however. If they bring the players or other children, have a designated, supervised area where they can go and play away from the parents.

I always preferred to conduct the meeting in a park where there is a pavilion with tables and an area where children can play.

STEP TWO: THE MEETING

Introduce Yourself

Tell the parents your name, your soccer experience, if any, and why you decided to coach this team.

> *What to say*: Good evening, I am John Smith. I was in youth soccer as a player, but this is my first time coaching soccer. I decided to coach because I enjoy soccer and I feel that I can teach your children the sport and have fun at the same time.

Parents Introduce Themselves

At this time the parents will just be sitting there looking at you. You need to get them involved right off the bat so they will relax. The best way to do this is to have them introduce themselves to you and to the rest of the team parents. You will not remember all of their names, but it's more important, at this time, to get them relaxed.

You will already have a list of the players' names and you can write the parents' names, beside the players' name, as they give them. Be alert for parents who have different last names than their children. Writing this down will enable you to call the parents by their correct names if you call them at home.

Ask the parents to give their names, their player's age, and the player's years of soccer playing experience, if any. Expect some of them to say more and some to say less. You may have to draw out the answers to actually get some of them to talk.

Tell the Parents What They Can Expect From You

Now that the parents have talked and relaxed a bit, it's time to move into what they can expect from you. This is why most of them came. This is your chance to convince them that you are in control. Keep the talk light, but be firm.

What to say: First of all, I am here to teach soccer to your children. Yes, I am the coach, but more than that I am their soccer teacher. I will teach them all aspects of the game. We'll do this and have fun too. It is difficult to pry children away from video games and TV, but my practices are designed to make the players enjoy themselves and look forward to coming to practice. I am not a "win at any cost coach." We will win some and lose some but we will get better every game.

I will encourage the players, not yell at or discourage them. Positive motivation is necessary to build strong players and strong individuals. Corrections will be made, but will be made constructively.

I will stay at the field until all of the players are picked up. If you have an emergency and are running late, don't worry about your child. If something happened and you know you are going to be late, just call me. I'll be giving you my cell phone number later in the meeting.

However, my time is valuable too. Practice does not end for me when the players leave the field. I still have to review the day's practice and set up the next. Help me by being on time or making arrangements for others to pick up your child.

Tell the Parents What You Expect From Them

This is the part where you establish the ground rules for the parents. Again, remember to keep it light, but be firm.

What to say: Since your children cannot drive themselves to practices or the games, I expect you to have them there on time. I will already have the practice schedule and drills established and all players are required to conduct the drills.

Also, if your player is late, they will miss out on valuable training. Being late to games also hurts the entire team by having to readjust the lineup to compensate for an absence. A lot of time goes into setting up a practice and establishing the players on the field to give the best possible lineup. Any last minute changes will distract from proper planning and penalizes the team as a whole. If you have a problem or know about other plans, please let me know ahead of time so I can make the necessary adjustments.

I also expect you to pick up your children on time. As I said, I will stay until you arrive, but I have a family and need to get home also. If you know ahead of time that you are going to be late, make arrangements to have your player picked up by someone else.

When the players are on the field, please do not yell instructions to them. We have already practiced what they need to do and I have already given them instructions. Other instructions will just confuse them.

Don't yell "pass the ball" or "shoot." They must also develop the ability to make their own decisions on the field. They need to develop their own techniques and they will learn by doing the action correctly and also by doing it wrongly. Yelling instructions and telling them what to do in every situation will hamper their ability to develop into good independent soccer players.

When you are sitting in the stands watching the game, yell only to encourage and motivate. This is very important and this is the way you can help develop your child into a better soccer player. If you want to yell, yell things like "good play," "nice try," or "way to go." When your child makes a good play they will look toward the stands to see if Mom or Dad, or Grandma or Grandpa saw the play before they will look at the coach. They are playing for your approval, and it's vital to their development. If you are positive in your interaction with your child, even when you have to dig deep to find something positive to say, your player will develop confidence and remain interested in trying.

During each game, pick out one good action and compliment your child on that action. Do something special like going some place your player likes, or getting an ice cream cone, as a reward for doing well.

It may also be beneficial to relate the following story to your parents—a story that comes from my personal experience:

What to say: I was once approached by a player's mother who stated that she didn't see anything her child did that she could compliment him on.

In truth, this player was afraid of the ball and stayed away from it as much as possible. I thought about the game and told her that on a couple of occasions her son got in the way of the person dribbling. I knew that her son was trying to get away from the ball, but he got in the way of the play. I told the mother to compliment the player on the fact that moving in front of the other players caused them to give up the ball, giving us the ball.

The player's mother did this, and took the player out for a banana split to celebrate the good play. The following week, the player was actually looking for someone to get in front of. The parent kept this up and by the end of the season this player had progressed into a decent soccer player.

A few other points worth covering:

What to say: Never offer money or other rewards for your player's on field performance. Don't say, "I will give you a dollar for every goal you make." Soccer is a team sport, and we don't want to promote individual achievement over team play. If players have this on their mind, they will shoot to get the money, even when they don't have a clear shot and should pass.

Remember, there are going to be good plays on both teams. It's okay to acknowledge this. When our players see others making new and good plays, they will try to imitate that action. That's good.

Be sure to always provide water for your child for the games and practices. They need to remain properly hydrated.

Help your child develop responsibility. Make them carry their own shoes, water, etc., from the car. Make them responsible for picking up their clothes and equipment after practice. Emphasizing this will enable them to develop the habit and become more responsible.

Everyone must abide by the rules. Soccer is a sport that encourages spectators to support their team, but does not tolerate any interference by players, coaches, or spectators. If anyone gets disruptive, I will ask that person to calm down. If the action continues, I will ask the referee to remove that person from the park. We have to show the children how to compete with sportsmanship. Outbursts and interference cannot be tolerated.

Team Manager

A team manager is one of the greatest assets you can have as a coach. This person does most of the off-field activities, allowing you to concentrate on the practices and games. This may not appear to be a great task at first blush, but after you have had to call all of the players two or three times to change practices due to bad weather, you begin to see that all of this is very time consuming. Some sports call this person the team mother. I never did, because I didn't need a mother for the team—I needed a manager, male or female.

What to say: I am looking for a volunteer to serve as the team manager. This person will assist me in the management of the team. Some of the things this person will be asked to do are: help with car pools or other ride arrangements, set schedules for drinks after the game and for oranges during halftime, set up and run fund-raisers, and help make calls to parents.

These aren't the only things the team manager does, but I can tell you, the team manager is one of the two most important helpers a coach can have.

NOTE: You will normally have at least one volunteer. If that doesn't happen, I normally fell to my knees and begged by saying, please, please, please. That always got a volunteer.

Assistant Coach

What to say: I also need an assistant coach. If you know soccer, or are willing to learn, I could really use your help. A coach must be on the practice and game field at all times. With two of us we can always ensure we have proper coverage for the players. Also, an assistant coach allows more information to be taught in a shorter amount of time.

Ask Parents to Talk to You

It is very important that the parents understand that they can talk to you at any time. Some will just want to complain, but having them complain to you is better than having them complain behind your back.

What to say: One item that I cannot over emphasize is that I want you to come to me if you have any questions, are not satisfied with something that is happening, or if your player will be late or miss the game or a practice.

The two major points of contention on any team are playing time and playing position. I know that some of you have already decided where you want your child to play.

I will put them in a position that is best suited for them and the team. That does not mean that they will be required to spend their whole life in that position.

Everyone will play. However, on some occasions some may play more than others. As they develop their skills, playing time will increase. The object is to develop and teach the players. I cannot do this with the players sitting on the bench, so I will work hard to develop everyone.

Ask Parents for Old Shirts

This is optional. Some coaches prefer to purchase a set of colored practice vests that the players can slip over their shirts. If you do not want to use the vest, just ask each parent to send an old white shirt to practice that you can dye. These will not be returned, so they don't need to send a good shirt.

What to say: Many of the practices will require the players to play as two teams. To be able to tell the two teams apart, I need to have two different colored shirts for the players to wear. I would like for you to send an old white shirt with your child to the first practice. I will take half of them and dye them so the players will have different color jerseys. These shirts will not be returned, so don't send anything new. Just make sure the shirt is serviceable.

Ask the Parents if Any of Them Have Medical Experience

It is good to know which, if any, of the parents on your team have medical experience. You may not find anyone, but it is good to check.

What to say: It is rare that a player gets hurt, but injuries do happen. Just in case an injury ever happens, is there anyone here who has formal medical experience?

If a person identifies him- or herself, ask, "Do you mind if I call upon you if we have an injury?"

Hand Out the Forms You Need the Parents to Complete

The organization will give you forms (medical, insurance, etc.) that need to be filled out by the parents. Do not hand these out until near the end. If you hand them out earlier, the parents will be looking at them rather than listening to you.

> *What to say*: I have a few forms that are needed by the league. These forms must be filled out prior to your child playing. Please fill them out and bring them back to me at the beginning of the first practice. If you have any questions, please call me.

Hand out the forms and include a slip of paper with your name, home number, work number, and cell phone number on it.

STEP THREE: CLOSING

> *What to say*: Before I close, I would like to thank all of you for coming tonight. I am looking forward to a fun, yet challenging season. Our practices will never be over an hour long, and we will only practice once or twice a week.
>
> Remember, all players must wear shin guards during all practices and games. They will not be allowed to play without them. Also they are required to wear athletic shoes or soccer shoes. Soccer shoes give them a better grip on the field and are recommended, but are not mandatory. If your children wear glasses, they must also wear a safety strap to hold the glasses on their heads. Please remove all jewelry from your child before practice and games so we don't waste time.
>
> "We will have our first practice on (day), at (0:00) PM, on the field located (directions).

SOLICIT VOLUNTEERS

One of the best things a parent can do is to become a volunteer to help. There are many ways they can be of assistance.

> *What to say*: All soccer organizations need referees. The leagues also do the training to qualify referees. You will never get rich, but you will make a little extra money, get some valuable exercise, and have fun.
>
> All organizations need people of different skills. They need people to help with the fields, administrative duties, and in many other areas. All you have to do is ask. They will be glad to hear from you.

9

Teaching Soccer

STAIR STEPS

Players learn better when they can progress from the most basic to advanced levels at their own speed. To do this, learning must have different levels of difficulty. I recommend using three different levels. They are progressive and are best taught in order of development.

I recommend using "B-I-A" because each letter directly relates to a skill level for each age between 4 and 8 years old. The letters B, I, and A, are identified with each drill to let you know the level of that skill and which ones to teach at which age. As the players progress in age they will also progress in the complexity of their skills and the drills they can perform. The actual skills needed, by age, are defined in chapter 13. Here are the definitions for B-I-A.

Basic (B)

This is the simplest set of skills, the lowest level of learning, and drills should focus on developing the basic soccer skills needed by each player. These basic skills are a necessity for every beginning soccer player.

Intermediate (I)

This is the next level of skills. It takes what was learned in the basics and makes those drills more difficult so your players are able to learn additional skills. These skills are just add-ons to the basic skills. This area ties the basic skills to the advanced skills. It is used as a stair step to develop the advanced skills.

Advanced (A)

Drills marked with the A are advanced skills needed for fully playing the game of soccer. These are the complete skills your players need to perform in all aspects of soccer.

Here is an example of B-I-A: Basic (B) dribbling is moving the ball from one place to another with control. Intermediate (I) dribbling is moving the ball from one place to another with control and the ability to move the ball right and left. Advanced (A) dribbling is moving the ball forward, to the right, and to the left, as well as stopping, backing up, and varying the speed.

INSTRUCTION

You have already spent years teaching your own child how to do things. You have taught them to tie their shoes, tell time, eat properly, and much more. Teaching the players on your team is very much the same. You are teaching them additional psychomotor or physical skills. The easiest way to do this is by using the techniques you are familiar with.

First you tell them "why" they need to do this, then "how" to do it, then "show" them how to do it, and then "practice doing it." You are using the same simple four-step approach that they have been using since they were born. Each skill area in this book is taught using a step-by-step approach. It is easy to follow for you and for the team. Remember, the younger the player, the shorter the attention span. Get them involved. Don't spend a lot of time lecturing or having them stand around while other players perform. Try to always have all players participating at the same time. Don't let your players stand in a line waiting to do something. They will get bored because it isn't fun.

Why?
Tell your players what they are going to learn and why they need to have the skill.

How?
This portion teaches the actual skill. In other words, how they do it.

Show
After your players know why they need to learn the skill and how to do it, they need to perform the actual skill. Although you are doing it with them, you are in reality showing them what they need to do. After you have gone through the learning of the drill, let them show you how they can do it. Compliment them. If they are doing it incorrectly, use positive motivation. Say things like "that was great, but remember to keep your ankle locked," or anything that tells them they are good and you are proud of them.

PRACTICE
This is where you use the drills designed to further enhance the skill they just learned. Try to watch your players rather than getting involved in the play. You must be able to see what they are doing to ensure that they are doing it correctly.

During the practice phase it is a must for you to correct them using specific criticism, while still encouraging them. This can be done by saying things like "that was great, but if you do X, Y and Z, it will be easier and better." When they do perform the skill correctly, you can then say, "That was done like a professional soccer player," or something as simple as, "That was really good." Praise is the greatest reward you can give a child who is learning something new.

Run as many basic drills as you need to enable them to learn the skill before moving up the skill stair step. At the end of every drill, let them know how well they did. There is no way to overemphasize how much your approval means to them.

10

Developing Your Players

CONDITIONING AND PERFORMANCE

If your players are not in proper condition to play the game of soccer, they will not do well and may also get hurt. They do not need to go to a gym and work out, but they do need to build up their ability to run and build their strength.

For young players to perform properly, they must possess the necessary skills. The skills are easy to teach and through simple and fun drills they can improve their performance. However, do not overdo the practice with your team. Keep it short and fun. Watch the games and concentrate on the areas that you players appear to be deficient in. The purpose of practice is to help your players improve while having fun. If you take your time and have patience, they will progress at a natural pace and their performance will steadily improve.

The best way to get into playing condition is through the development of aerobic fitness. This is a combination of exercises that builds the player's cardiovascular endurance and muscular fitness. Your players must be able to run continuously while also performing actions involving different muscle groups.

Don't forget to stop for regular water breaks to prevent dehydration in your players. Don't stop based upon when you are thirsty. You may not be running as much as your players, so keep a close watch and give them breaks often.

OUTCOME OF AEROBIC FITNESS

Duration
Players must be properly fit to participate in the game. They cannot stop moving while on the field and must be conditioned to last the whole game. If your team participates in tournaments, the duration of play is extended over multiple games.

Agility
Your players must be able to start, stop, and change directions quickly.

Strength and Power
Leg power must be developed. The game of soccer requires running, jumping, stopping quickly, and starting quickly.

Speed
The game of soccer covers a wide spectrum of running. It incorporates full-on running, slow movement to full acceleration, and stopping.

Mental Reaction
This is a byproduct of proper aerobic fitness. The more fit the body, the easier it is for your player to be able to think while in competition or in a workout.

11

Practice Setup

Proper preparation is important to ensure that your practices are conducted with maximum effect and efficiency.

There are many things that have to be done, but much of it can be done ahead of time to ensure that you do not impact your practices or inhibit your time and attention at a game. Normally practices for U-6 and U-8 teams do not go beyond one hour and are held no more than once or twice per week. Most teams will practice twice a week prior to the start of the season and then go to one practice a week once the games start. Check your organization's bylaws. Practice time might be limited to a specific time and a certain number of practices per week. Practice numbers and times can increase with the older players.

PRE-PRACTICE PREPARATION

Your practices need to be conducted so they are productive and fun. Your players will look forward to coming to practices and participating in them if the practices are run smoothly, they learn new skills or improve existing ones, and they have fun. To ensure this happens, certain goals need to be accomplished prior to the first practice.

PRACTICE SCHEDULE PRIOR TO START OF THE SEASON

Make an outline of what you want to accomplish during your upcoming season. Look at a calendar and write down how many practices you have available between the start of practices and the start of games. Decrease this number by at least one to count for rain outs or other bad weather.

List the days and dates, then for every night of practice list one or two skills that you want to teach. Below the skill headings list the drills you want the players to do. List these on the schedule. This will ensure that you will have the players prepared by the start of the season. Remember, the schedule is fluid. If you get ahead or behind your schedule, you can easily adjust it.

Sample Practice Schedule (60 Minutes)
Warm-up: 5 minutes
Conditioning: 10 minutes
Water break: 1 minute
Drill: 10 minutes
Water break: 1 minute
Drill: 15 minutes
Water break: 1 minute
Drill: 15 minutes
Water break/End of practice: 2 minutes

Arriving for Practice
Arrive early for practice so you have time to set up the field for the skills or drills you want to work on that day. Every practice must have an objective. Remember you do not have a lot of time to practice, so maximizing your practice time is a must.

When you are working with U-6, the best you can hope for is to teach the basic skills they will use in their games. These are: dribbling, shooting/passing, receiving, the throw-in, the goal kick, the corner kick, and defending the ball. Moving into U-8, you can then work on all of the skills and teach formational play. In U-6 the only formation is to keep the few players on the field separated.

Practice Schedule Once the Season Begins

Once you have started playing the games, make out another schedule. This schedule will only cover a one-week period. After each game, schedule practice time for the areas in which you feel your team requires additional work.

Throughout the season, you will be able to again cover all of the skills and aspects of the game. By listing the areas in need of improvement and the drills you want the players to complete, you can run a productive practice and ensure that the players improve.

Week	Skill/Drill Improvement Area	Skill/Drill Improvement Area	Skill/Drill Improvement Area
Practice 1			
Practice 2			
Practice 3			

Figure 11.1. Skill/Drill Practice Schedule

CONDUCTING YOUR PRACTICE

The following activities are designed for all of the players on your team. Remember: don't use drills that leave the players standing in line waiting. Get every player involved at the same time, in every drill you run.

The first step is having the teams do exercises. These are good for everyone, including you. Exercising along with your players helps you better understand the difficulty or ease of what your players are trying to do. Information and tactics are specifics of the game that can be discussed as you conduct the training sessions. Overall, by doing these with your team you get in better shape, learn techniques, and develop a better understanding of the game of soccer.

Practice can be held in an open field, a local park, a schoolyard, or any place that is convenient and has a grass area for playing. It can be done on the street or parking lot, but is much better if you can find a grassy area.

When you are working with your team you need to be consistent in your approach. This develops good workout habits. Always start the practice with activities that enable your players to warm up. However, do not spend more than five or ten minutes on warm-up. Don't skip the warm-up because your players have been in school all day or have been playing with their friends. They need to warm up for the soccer drills that you are getting ready to run. There are different ways you can do this.

Any warm-up activity that allows players to stretch their muscles is good. A side benefit is developing muscles that are used in the game of soccer. Also, remember you are much larger than the players on your team and you should refrain from playing against any of your team. You need to watch what they are doing so you can ensure that they are doing it correctly.

The second area that you need to address is the actual teaching or reinforcement of a learned skill. Teaching is done by using established guidelines and information. Reinforcement of the skill is done by running fun drills.

Most skills are taught to a certain age group and that age group does well learning the skills. If your players are having trouble performing a skill, back up and be patient. If the activity is easy for the players, challenge them by running more advanced skills or drills.

ACTUAL PRACTICE SCHEDULES (60 MINUTES)

Use this actual practice schedule, adding or deleting activities as needed. Just cut out what your team has already learned and add the skills that still need to be taught, then put in the drills needed for support. As the players advance in age, many of the drills should incorporate multiple skills into a single activity. Don't forget to add a small amount of scrimmage time into each practice. Kids always want to play the game of soccer, not just run drills.

First Practice
Warm-up: 5 minutes
Conditioning: 10 minutes
Drills: dribbling, 15 minutes
Drills: shooting/passing, 15 minutes
Scrimmage: 10 minutes
Water breaks: 5 minutes total

Second Practice
Warm-up: 5 minutes
Conditioning: 10 minutes
Drills: dribbling, shooting/passing, 15 minutes

Drills: throw-in, one segment, 15 minutes
Scrimmage: 10 minutes
Water breaks: 5 minutes total

Third Practice
Warm-up: 5 minutes
Conditioning: 10 minutes
Drills: shooting/passing, one segment, 10 minutes (You can choose drills that also include dribbling.)
Drills: corner kick, goal kick, one segment, 15 minutes
Drills/Scrimmage: kickoff, one segment, 15 minutes (Switch your players so each get to kickoff and each get to try and capture the ball.)
Water breaks: 5 minutes total

Fourth Practice
Warm-up: 5 minutes
Conditioning: 10 minutes
Drills: throw-in, one segment, 10 minutes
Drills: combination, dribbling, shooting/passing, corner and goal kicks, and kickoff, 15 minutes
Scrimmage: 15 minutes
Water breaks: 5 minutes total

After the fourth practice you will have covered everything your team will need in order to compete in their first game. They won't be professional players, but they will have a basic understanding of what is expected of them. If they have that, you will be well on your way to having a really good season.

If you still have practice time before the start of the season, work on dribbling, shooting/passing, and other skills as time permits. Once the games start, concentrate your practices on areas in which you feel your team needs to improve.

Remember, it is normally okay to hold two practices a week prior to the start of the season, but once the games start, practicing once a week is sufficient. You may have games during the week. If you do, this game counts as your practice. These young players are not professional and too much soccer too soon can burn them out.

12

Starting Each Practice (Warm-Up)

RUNNING DRILLS

Make sure each player has his or her own ball. When they are doing running drills, try having them run with and dribble the ball as much as they can.

Running is very good for building strength and endurance. However, just running is boring to small children, so you will need to find a way to make the running fun for them. It is best done with the ball since the player learns to dribble and develops touch on the ball. Make it interesting by going around trees, bleachers, goals, or whatever is on or around your practice field. Speed is not required. Running fast before the players are warmed up can lead to injuries.

What You Need: A soccer ball for each player and an area to run and dribble.

How to Do It: The first time your team does this, walk them through the area in which they will be running/dribbling. After they know where they will be going, let them start dribbling as they run the course. Make sure they do not run too fast. Also make sure they maintain control of the ball. Repeat run area as required.

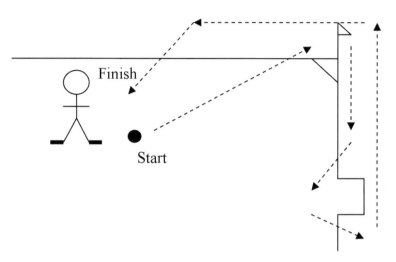

Figure 12.1. Running—Warm Up

Knee Lift Running

This conditions your player to running and also stretches and develops muscle groups used in soccer.

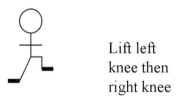

Lift left knee then right knee

Figure 12.2. Knee Lift Running

What You Need: Have each player run the same path they ran in the running drill, but this time without the ball.

How to Do It: Have your players lift their knees as they run. The knee should come up to the waist level. It is much like skipping, but the main focus should be on keeping them moving while they lift their knees in the air. You as the coach need to watch and encourage the players to keep moving and lifting their knees.

Running Anywhere

This drill develops fitness, balance, agility, and dribbling. A byproduct is it that allows independent thinking. This is a running and dribbling drill that allows your players to use their imagination. The drill is fun and allows them to make decisions while developing their running ability and dribbling skills. Anything goes in this drill. Encourage your player to be creative.

What You Need: Each player needs their own soccer ball.

How to Do It: Have each player place a ball on the ground and start dribbling. They can dribble anywhere they want. Use your whistle to have them stop. Tell them to step over the ball and dribble in the opposite direction. Stop them again and have them move sideways, nudging the ball as they move. They can also push the ball with their head, do somersaults, bunny hop as they run, and stand on their head, etc. They are only limited by your imagination. If you can't think of things to do, ask you players. After a while they will be able to come up with their own creations.

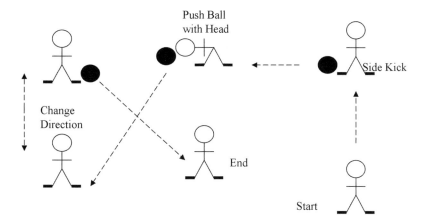

Figure 12.3. Running Anywhere

CONDITIONING DRILLS

After your players have done a few running drills, it is time to stretch their muscles and also to condition their muscles. Direct the exercises by doing them along with your team. This way you and your team both get exercise, and it's also easier for the players if they can see it being done.

Stretching

There are many ways to stretch. However, your players must do static stretches only, which means they must reach out and hold that position. There is no bouncing or moving back and forth.

Start with each player sitting on the ground. Have them spread their legs out in front of them, and to the side as far as they can and still be comfortable. Then have them lean toward the right or left leg, placing their head on their knee. Have them hold that position for at least five seconds. If players cannot touch their knee, have them bend as far as they can.

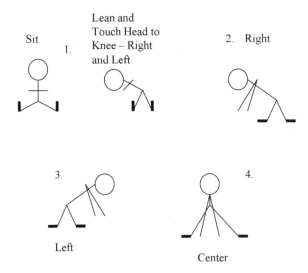

Figure 12.4. Stretching

After your players have done this to the right and left two or three times, have them stand up. Have them spread their legs and lean down and to the left, trying to touch their toes with their hands. Ask them to repeat this to the right and then the center. When touching in the center, have the player reach down and back, in between their legs. Just have them reach as far as they can and still remain comfortable.

Leg Lift and Jump

Have you players stand straight up and face you. Then tell them to lift one of their legs up behind them. They can hold their leg in position with their hand. The heel of their foot will be touching their backside and their knee will be pointing straight down. You can tell them they are like a stork because they are standing on one leg.

When the player is standing on just one leg, have them look out away from themselves to an area at least four feet in front of them. That will help them keep their balance. Looking down at their foot that is on the ground will cause them to have trouble maintaining their balance.

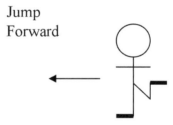

Figure 12.5. Leg Lift and Jump

Once they are on one leg have them jump forward on that leg. Start with just a few jumps and build up as they are able to control their balance.

Ball Dancing

This skill will be slow to develop and will take much practice, but it is worth the effort. It helps to develop balance, coordination, agility, and touch and is a good fitness drill as well.

Have your players place the ball on the ground in front of them. They are going to be touching the ball with the bottoms of their feet. Have them only use the bottoms of their feet underneath their toes. Tap the ball very gently so as not to move the ball. Tap it with the right foot while the left foot is on the ground and then the left foot with the right foot placed on the ground. Have them drop their foot back to the ground between touches on the ball. The ball and ground touches will be very short.

When your players first start, don't worry about speed. Concentrate on technique. As your players become more comfortable, have them pick up their speed until they can dance with the ball really fast. After they get good, have them move around the ball as they dance with it.

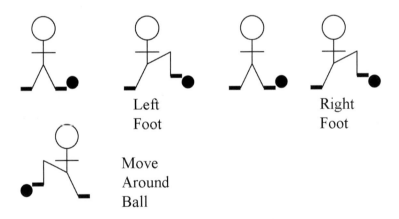

Left
Foot

Right
Foot

Move
Around
Ball

Figure 12.6. Ball Dancing

Frog Jump

Have each player put the ball between their legs so it is tight against the inside of their legs and feet. Then have them jump and pull the ball up as they jump. This builds leg strength.

Figure 12.7. Frog Jump

Jump and Volley

This builds balance, leg strength, and teaches the players to volley. Have each player line up in a straight line in front of you. Have them jump forward with one leg in the air, landing on one leg. After they land and gain their balance, throw the ball underhanded and have them volley, or kick, the ball back to you. Move rapidly down the line and let the players go get the ball they kicked. Have them jump and stand on the right and left leg, and volley with the opposite foot. If you have an assistant coach, split the team in half so more kicks can be accomplished in a short timeframe.

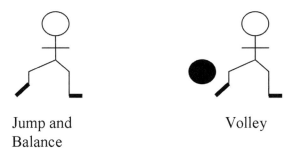

Figure 12.8. Jump and Volley

ALTERNATE CONDITIONING DRILLS

These are additional conditioning drills that you can have your team do. Some of these require lying on the ground. Only use them if the field you are practicing on does not have stickers or a lot of red ants.

Figure 12.9. Spider

Spider

Have players lie flat on their stomach and then push themselves up until they are balancing on their legs and arms. Have them move like a spider by moving their legs and arms separately and then together. To do it together, have them move their right arm and right leg together, and then their left arm and left leg together. This is fun and stretches their arm, leg, back, and stomach muscles.

Upside-Down Crawl

Have your players lie on their backs and then, using their arms and legs, have them push themselves up and away from

Figure 12.10. Upside Down Crawl

the ground. After they are up off the ground, have them move forward and backward using their arms and legs.

Wheelbarrow

This is fun for players and stretches and builds their muscles. Have half of the players lay down on the ground, face down. Place the soccer ball near their head. Have the other half of the players pick up their teammates' feet. The players on the ground will then push themselves up with their arms. Have them walk forward using their arms while the person holding their feet in the air follows where they go. They will move like a wheelbarrow while they push the ball with their head.

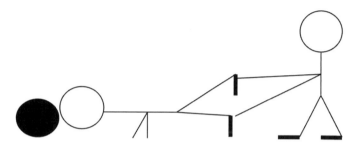

Figure 12.11. Wheelbarrow

Jumping Rope

This provides fitness, leg strength, and timing. Give players a jump rope and then have them stand with the rope in their hands, in a position to jump rope. Now, have them place the ball between their legs, clamping onto the ball or holding the ball by forcing pressure against it with both legs. Now have them swing the rope and start jumping the rope, while still holding the ball. This is a bit difficult when players first try it, but they will quickly be able to jump the rope and hold the ball at the same time.

Figure 12.12.
Jumping Rope

Line Hopping

This provides fitness, endurance, and leg strength. Place at least five cones in a straight line about one or two feet apart. Have each player jump from the side of one cone to the side of the next cone. As they are able to easily jump and land next to the cone, increase the distance of the cones. Have them go back and forth jumping for at least one set away from you and one set toward you.

After they have completed the two sets, let them rest. This is a type of interval training. Interval training is moving quickly and then resting a short duration and then repeating the exercise. As your players build their strength, increase the number of times they jump. This builds endurance.

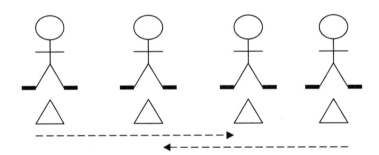

Jump From One Cone To The Other

Figure 12.13. Line Hopping

Toss and Kick

This builds leg strength and limited fitness. Have your players lie on their backs and draw their feet up to their chest. Throw the ball to their feet and have them kick the ball back to you using the sole of their shoe. This can be done using the right foot, left foot, or both feet.

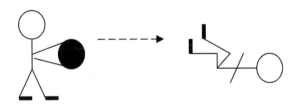

Figure 12.14. Toss and Kick

13

Practice Skills
and Drills

Learning the skills and then performing drills to improve those skills is essential to the development of all young players. Remember, different age groups require different levels of skills. The players need to move into the advanced skills, but only after they have become proficient at the basic and intermediate levels.

Under each different skill in the "why" area below is an explanation of the basic, intermediate, and advanced skills needed. They are also listed by age. You may find that you want to increase the level or decrease the level depending on your players' abilities. You do not have to follow the age recommendations if they don't apply. To let you know what skills are needed and at what age, they are listed below and repeated again in the skills sections that follow.

SKILLS NEEDED BY AGE GROUP
Age 4: basic dribbling, basic shooting, and standing throw-in
Age 5: basic dribbling, basic shooting, standing throw-in, and basic receiving

Age 6: intermediate dribbling, intermediate shooting, standing throw-in, intermediate receiving, basic shielding, basic heading, and basic juggling

Age 7: intermediate dribbling, intermediate shooting/passing, standing throw-in, intermediate receiving, intermediate shielding, intermediate juggling, intermediate heading, and possibly goal keeping

Age 8: advanced everything: dribbling, shooting/passing, moving throw-in, receiving, shielding, heading, volleys, juggling, and possibly goal keeping

DRIBBLING

Why?

Dribbling is one of the most important aspects of soccer. Dribbling is how your players move the ball around the field while maintaining control of it. To get to the goal in a position to score, they must dribble. This is one of the fundamental skills each player must learn.

Dribbling is accomplished by pushing or kicking the ball with the feet. Most dribbling is done with soft taps to the ball; however, if your player is in open field and no one is near, the ball can be pushed farther away to increase speed, as long as it is not so far away that he or she loses control.

> *NOTE:* Most young players, when learning to dribble, kick the ball and run to it. Do not let your players do that. It is a bad habit to start. Your players must keep the ball close enough to maintain control. Control is defined as keeping the ball and not allowing an opposing player to get it away from you.

Basic: Moving the ball forward and moving their heads up to look where they are going. Ages 4 and 5.

Intermediate: Moving the ball using their toe, inside, and outside of foot. Ages 6 and 7.

Advanced: Moving the ball with all parts of the foot, using the sole of their shoe to pull the ball back, and turning the ball with the inside and outside of their foot. Age 8.

How?

1. When players are dribbling, they need to watch the ball when they touch it but also keep their head up so they can see the goal (where their own teammates are) and the opposing players. This is hard for them to do at first and will take time. They will want to watch the ball and not anything else. Work with them so they look where they are going. Be patient, because this is an essential skill of the game.

2. Your players should push the ball forward using the tops or sides of their feet, but not their toes. Unless they are running in the clear with no defenders challenging, your players should touch the ball every time they take a step. They will need to keep the ball close to them to accomplish this.

3. Tell your players to dribble away from people to get to an open place where they can dribble without other players hampering their moves. Moving to open space also enables them to pass, though most U-6 players will find it difficult to pass the ball to another player. Once they have the ball the likelihood is that they are going to keep it. Work with your team on passing but don't get discouraged if it's a slow process. It will develop over time.

4. To be an effective dribbler, your players must learn to vary their dribbling speed. This is seldom if ever done in U-6 soccer. It will start in U-8 soccer and they will need to learn how to move laterally in fake movements. This will make it look as if

they are going to go in one direction while they are actually moving in another.

5. Your players may use their insteps, the tops of their feet, or the outside of their feet to dribble and change direction.

6. When your players are dribbling they will need to avoid other players to maintain possession. They must learn how to dribble the ball away from the other players.

7. As soon as your player gets open and they can see open teammates, have them pass the ball. This is something that you can work on, but it will take time.

Note: Remember the designations used to denote the level of the skills being taught are:

B = Basic
I = Intermediate
A = Advanced

Basic Dribbling (B)

What You Need: This drill uses a ball for each player and two cones to mark out an area.

How to Do It: The object of this drill is to teach each player the proper techniques used to dribble. If your players already know how to dribble properly, move on to the next drill. If your players cannot dribble using both feet as they run, they need to do this drill.

Set up the two cones. One is to mark the starting point of the drill and one is to mark the end. Starting with just the right foot, have your players push the ball with the tops of their feet, using the area from their toe to their laces, to move the ball to the other cone. Do not let them dribble flat-footed. They need to be on their toes. After they have gone back and forth a few times just using the right foot, have them repeat the drill just using their left foot.

The next part of the drill is to have your players dribble back and forth using both feet. Make sure they touch the soccer ball every step using the foot closest to the ball. Do not let them stutter-step to use a particular foot instead of the closest foot to the ball.

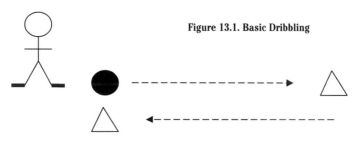

Figure 13.1. Basic Dribbling

Three Steps: 1. Right Foot, 2. Left Foot, and 3. Both Feet

Through the Cone Races (B)

What You Need: This drill uses a ball for each player and numerous cones to mark out an area.

How to Do It: This object of this drill is to teach your players to dribble while maintaining control of the soccer ball. Set up cones in a straight or jagged line. Make enough lines for all players to have their own. Space some cones far away from each other so your players can also learn control.

Blow your whistle to start the race. Have your players dribble through the cones and then turn around and dribble back. This is fun and allows the players to compete against each other.

Another way to do this drill is to split your players into two teams of three or four players and have each team race against the other. When you name the teams, do not use team 1 and team 2. Children know at a very early age that it's better to be number 1. Use something like A or B, animal names, uniform colors like blue and white, or cartoon characters as the names for the teams.

This is also a very good way to balance your players. Select the teams and have them do a relay race. The first player dribbles through the cones, and after he or she returns, the second player takes off. Keep this up until all of the players have made it through the cones.

As the players race, pick out the players who are the best. Some will be faster and have better ball control than the others. Rearrange the teams by splitting the two best players and run the race again. Keep moving the players until the two teams are evenly matched and it's a toss up as far as who will win. At that point you will probably have the two teams you will use during the game, as it should give you two teams that are evenly balanced.

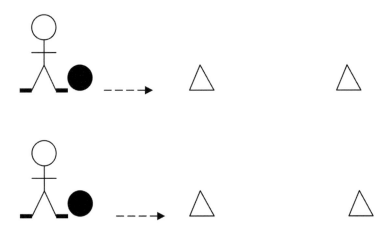

Figure 13.2. Through the Cones Races

Circle Dribble (I)

What You Need: This drill uses a ball for each player and numerous cones to mark out a circle area.

How to Do It: The object of this drill is to teach your players to dribble while changing their speed and direction. Use cones to mark out a dribbling area for your players. Have your players dribble outside the cone going clockwise and then have them go around the outside of the cones counterclockwise. After they are able to control the ball while dribbling, have them move in and out of the cones.

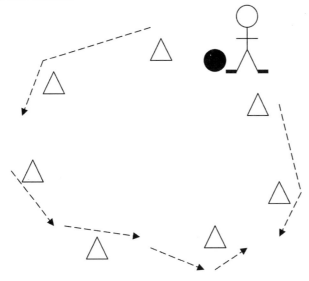

Figure 13.3. Circle Dribble

You're It (I)

What You Need: This drill uses all players, each with a ball, and numerous cones to mark out an area.

How to Do It: The object of this drill is to teach your players to dribble while simultaneously changing speed and direction and keeping the ball away from the opponent. Using cones, mark out a border area for your players. Designate one person as "it." That person has to dribble his or her own ball while the other players are dribbling their balls. The person that is "it" dribbles and when they reach out and touch another player, that player yells out, "You're it!" Now the new "it" must try to touch another player while dribbling.

Let them make their own decisions on what movements to make and whom to touch. The players will try to touch or get away by leaving their ball and moving. Tell your players to keep control of the ball while they dribble.

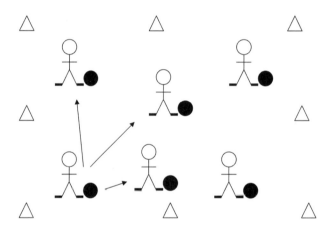

Figure 13.4. You're It

Getting Past the Monster (I)

What You Need: This drill uses all players. Each player has a ball, except the monster. Use cones to mark the limits.

How to Do It: The object of this drill is to teach your players to dribble while someone is trying to take the ball away from them. Use two sets of cones to mark an area where the monster stands. The monster must stay inside this area but can move anywhere inside of it. All of the other players must try to dribble past the monster to get to the other side. The monster's job is to kick their ball away as they come through his or her area.

If the monster kicks the ball away the player who lost the ball becomes an additional monster. The players who make it past the monster now come back the opposite direction they originally came. Keep this up until only one player still has a ball. Then have the players go get their own balls, select a new monster, and do it again.

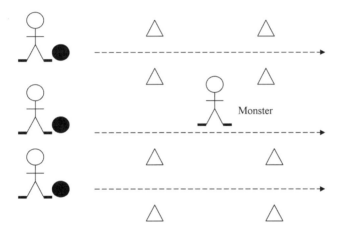

Figure 13.5. Getting Past the Monster

Driving the Ball (A)

What You Need: This drill uses all players, each with a ball. Line up the players even with each other and facing you. Use cones to mark the limits.

How to Do It: With all of the players lined up, yell out and tell them to drive. They start dribbling the ball. Yell out "turn" and point in a direction. They must look at you to see which way you are pointing. During the drill give other commands, like "red light," which means they have to stop and put their foot on the ball. To start again, yell "green light." When you yell "back up," they will have to roll the ball with the sole of their shoe to move backward and also make a beeping noise to let the other drivers know they are backing up. "Parking" is when they move the ball right or left using the inside and outside of their foot.

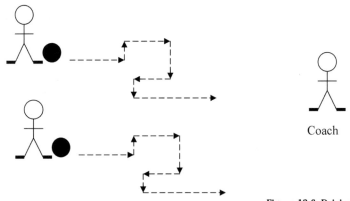

Coach

Figure 13.6. Driving the Ball

PASSING

Most under-6 players will have a hard time passing the ball. It isn't because passing is difficult, but because once they get the ball they have one thought on their mind, and that is to dribble and shoot. Passes to another player may seldom occur, but you do need to work to have your players learn to pass the ball, as it is an essential skill of the game.

Every player has a best kick portion on his or her foot. The best-hit spot is referred to as a sweet spot. (This term is used in other sports too. In tennis, the racket is said to have a sweet spot, a place where hits result in the best consistent action.)

Before you start to teach passing or shooting, it is best to find the sweet spot on each player's foot. To find this spot, here are the steps to follow:

1. Sit your players down, placing the soles of their shoes on the ground in front of them.
2. Have them move their feet back toward their body, without resting them against their body.
3. Have your players hold the ball above their foot and then drop the ball straight down.
4. As the ball is coming down, have your players bring their foot up to meet the ball while it is in the air. The ankle must be locked for this action to work. The foot cannot flop up and down.
5. When the ball is struck by the top of their shoe, the ball will bounce straight back up in the air.
6. Ask your players to remember where the ball hit on their foot. If the ball goes straight up without spin, you have found the sweet spot. The sweet spot will normally be on the laces of the shoe. Mark that spot (with chalk or tape), as it is the area that will allow them to execute the most accurate passes and shots.
7. If the ball spins forward, the ball hit too high on their foot. If the ball spins backwards toward your player, it hit too near their toe.

NOTE: Passing can be done with the instep, top of the foot, outside of the foot, heel, or sole of the shoe. Practice all different types of passes. However, do not let players kick with their toe. Accuracy cannot be achieved using the toe. The reason is very simple: if the kick is with the toe and happens to be kicked perfectly on the tip of the shoe, it will go straight. If the kick is just to the right of center, the soccer ball will go right, and if the strike is just left of center, the ball will be propelled left. No one can kick accurately with the toe. Start your players kicking correctly and reinforce the proper methods.

Why?

There is a difference between passing and shooting the ball. Passing is how you get the ball from one player to another. Shooting is when you kick the ball toward or into the goal. The same basic technique is used, but shooting is taught separately.

You must pass the ball to the feet of the other player. If it is not accurate, the other team's players can get the ball. The more accurate your players' passes are, the better players they will be.

Basic: Use the laces of the shoe or the instep of the shoe to pass the ball to another player or into the goal. Ages 4 and 5.

Intermediate: Use both feet to pass the ball using the laces, instep, and outside of the foot. Ages 6 and 7.

Advanced: Use the laces, inside, outside, heel, and bottom of the foot to pass the ball to a teammate. Pass and then move to open space to receive the ball. Age 8.

How?

1. Have your players stand directly over the ball. They must be balanced. They will have to lift their kicking leg so that the knee of that leg is pointing downward toward the ball and the foot is up and behind them.
2. The leg that is not being used to kick the ball will be planted next to the ball.
3. The toe of their plant foot must remain pointed in the direction the pass or shot is intended to go. When the ball is kicked, the direction the plant foot is pointing is the direction the ball will travel.
4. The ankle of the foot kicking the ball must be held firm. In other words, it must be locked into place. This is true every time the ball is struck, whether it be a pass or a shot.
5. The player must look up at where they want to pass, and then back at the ball so their eyes are on the ball at the time of the kick.

6. As the foot swings toward the ball, the orientation of the kicking foot needs to be horizontal with the toe elevated slightly, and locked, so the instep of the foot strikes the face of the ball.

7. When the foot strikes the ball, the foot and leg must not stop moving. The momentum of the kick should cause the foot to connect with the ball and carry the ball all the way through the kick. Never stop the straight motion of the kick when the ball is hit with the foot. It is important that the foot follows through the ball, completing the kicking motion.

8. Remember, the pass can be made with the top of the foot, the instep, the outside, or the heel of the foot. The sole of the shoe can be used to roll the ball backward.

Kicking Practice

A proven way to practice kicking a soccer ball is to place the ball in some kind of bag. This is a good way to get maximum kicks in a short period of time. The players can do this at practice or they can do it when they are at home. Kicking the ball against the house, backyard fence, etc., or kicking to another person, limits the kicks. More can be accomplished in minutes with a bag than in hours with other people. You can use a pillowcase, a plastic bag, or anything else that will hold the ball. To do this:

1. Drop the ball into the bag.
2. Have the player close the top of the bag and then hold onto the top of the bag.
3. The player kicks the ball while it is in the bag. This can be done while standing still, walking forward, or running.
4. Have your player kick the ball continuously using the top of the foot, the instep, and outside of the foot. Make sure they alternate feet when kicking.

5. When using the top of the foot, you will be able to tell if it is a good kick by the way the ball travels away from the kick. If the ball and the bag go to the side or the bag twists, it is a bad kick. If it goes straight out and back, it is a good kick. When using the instep, the ball will travel away from the instep. When using the outside of the foot, the ball will travel away from the kick.

Golf Kick (B)

What You Need: Place multiple cones around the field, anywhere you want. Give each of your players a soccer ball.

How to Do It: This drill teaches your players to pass and shoot accurately, teaches them to touch on the ball, and enables them to establish kicking strength to determine distance. It is also a fun game. Designate a starting point for your players. This can change every time you do the drill. That way it will be different every time.

Number the cones using sticky notes, mark each cone with a permanent marker, or just tell your players which one is the next one in line. Have your players kick the ball at the cone. Make sure they pass using their instep, top of foot, and outside of foot.

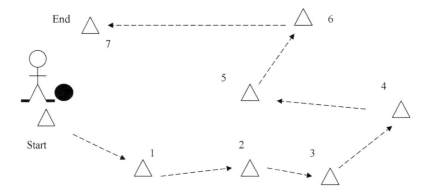

Figure 13.7. Golf Kick

Have each player go separately. Each follows the first person and goes in the same sequence. Have your players concentrate on accuracy. Every time a player kicks the ball, it counts as a kick or a count. The object is to hit all of the cones with the ball, with the fewest number of kicks. The lower the score, the better. Have the players try to beat their own score, or if competing against another player, have them try to end with the fewest number of kicks.

Carnival Kick (B)

What You Need: Multiple cones set up in parallel rows with one player behind each. Only one ball for each two players is needed.

How to Do It: This drill teaches players to pass and shoot accurately, use proper passing techniques, and build passing strength. Set the distance between the two sets of cones according to the strength of your players. It is best to start close so the player can have success, and then move them farther apart

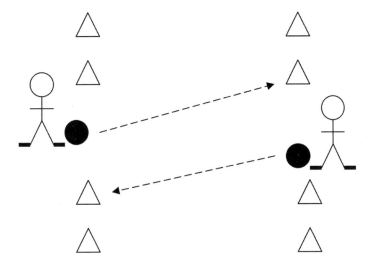

Figure 13.8. Carnival Kick

as your players improve. Make sure they pass using their instep, top of foot, and outside of foot. Let all of the players on one side kick first, starting the drill.

The object is to knock all of their cones down before the other side can knock theirs down. Once a cone is knocked down, it stays down and the player must concentrate on the standing cones only. The person who knocks down all of the cones first is the winner. This is like throwing a ball at milk bottles at a carnival. Knocking them all down is the goal.

Back and Forth (I)

What You Need: Two cones centered between two people. Also place one cone at each kicking spot to show players where to stand. Space the center cones about three feet apart. Only one ball is required.

How to Do It: This drill teaches your players to pass and kick accurately, and also teaches your players to move to receive the pass. Place a person on each side of the center cones, standing next to a kicking cone. The object is to pass to the other person, but with the ball going through the center cones. Make sure your players pass using their instep, top of foot, and outside of foot. Increase the distance or pass at angles to the center cones as the players improve.

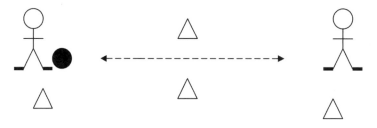

Figure 13.9. Back and Forth

Monster in the Middle (I)

What You Need: A soccer ball for every two players and numerous cones to mark a center space.

How to Do It: Place the cones so they are in two parallel lines with four to five feet between each line of cones. Split the players so half of them are on one side and half on the other side of the set of cones. Give a ball to the players on one side, and while you are in the middle of the cones, have those players pass to the other players on the far side of the cones. Be sure to designate who passes to whom. While in the middle, keep moving so the players have to pass around you. Purposely miss the ball so the players can keep passing. The objective of this drill is to teach accuracy, to pass away from other players, and to have the person receiving the ball move to receive it.

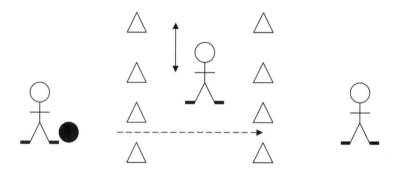

Figure 13.10. Monster in the Middle

Hit the Ball (I)

What You Need: Give each player a ball. You will also need one extra ball and some cones to mark the center area and the shooting point.

How to Do It: This drill is teaches your players to focus on passing accuracy and distance. Split the team in two. Take the extra ball and put it between the two teams. Start with a distance of about ten feet between the players and the ball. The object of the game is for players to pass their own ball and hit the center ball, knocking it into the other team's area.

The other team will be trying to hit the center ball in the other direction. Have all the players pass at the same time and then go get their balls, go back to the passing line, and do it again. Set a time limit of a few minutes. The team that knocks the center ball into the other team's area wins. Repeat this drill.

The ball in the center should be a size-5 ball or a ball that is somehow distinguishable from the others. You can take a normal ball and put stickers on it, draw smiley faces on it, or use a ball that has a color that makes it different from the other balls. This teaches accuracy, gets the players running after their balls, and is a lot of fun.

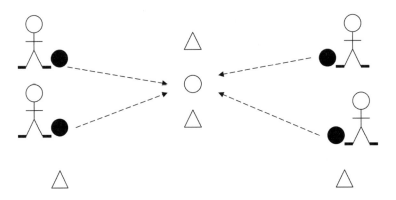

Figure 13.11. Hit the Ball

Deflect Ball (A)
What You Need: This drill uses you, one ball for each player, and cones.

How to Do It: This drill teaches your players to pass the ball, move to the ball, receive the ball, and dribble the ball. Stand with your back to the goal and move about five yards away from it. Have your players stand in front of you, facing you, three yards away. Have your first player pass the ball directly to your feet. Use your foot to redirect the ball to your right or left side.

As your players kick the ball, have them move toward you. As you kick the ball, they will move in the direction of the ball. When they catch up to the ball they will pass it to hit the cones set up as the target. Make sure the player passes using the instep, top of foot, and outside of foot. As soon as you have deflected the first ball, have the second player pass and keep them moving. Use your assistant coach to form two groupings if possible.

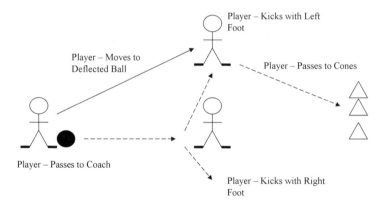

Figure 13.12. Deflect Ball

Start by having your players pass the ball using the one touch method. This means they do not dribble. They pass the soccer ball as soon as they reach it. For the next repetition of the drill have your players move to the ball, dribble it toward the target cones, and then pass, knocking over the cones.

To make this a U-8 drill, put a goalkeeper in the goal and ask your players to take a shot on goal after receiving their deflected pass.

Turn Around and Pass (A)

What You Need: This drill requires three players and two balls.

How to Do It: The purpose of this drill is to teach your players to listen to other players on the field, quickly locate the ball, receive, and pass, using both feet.

Line up three players in a straight line. The two players on the outside will be facing each other and will each have a ball. The player in the center faces toward one of the outside players. It doesn't matter which one. Make sure each player is approximately three yards away from the others.

Have the player with the ball slowly pass it directly to the feet of the player in the center. As soon as he or she passes, that player must yell and tell the center player to turn. As the center player turns, he or she will quickly focus on the ball, move to receive the ball, and then pass the ball back to you.

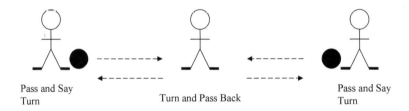

Pass and Say
Turn

Turn and Pass Back

Pass and Say
Turn

Figure 13.13. Turn Around and Pass

Make sure your player passes the ball using the instep, top of foot, or outside of foot. This can be done as a one touch where your player kicks the ball straight back without stopping the ball, or by receiving the ball and then passing it.

As soon as the center player passes the ball back, the player on the other side passes the ball and yells "turn." This drill can be done very quickly and your players can do at least twenty reps before they start to tire.

SHOOTING

Why?

Everyone wants to score a goal, but to do this your players must know how to shoot the ball where they want it to go and with the correct amount of strength. Shooting, or kicking the ball to the goal, may be a very hard shot or a shot that is just tapped into the goal. Accuracy is a must to get it into the goal, past the goalkeeper.

Basic: Kick the ball using the laces or instep of the foot. Ages 4 and 5.

Intermediate: Kick the ball accurately using the laces or instep of the foot. Ages 6 and 7.

Advanced: Kick the ball accurately and with the proper strength using the laces or instep of the foot. Age 8.

How?

1. The procedure for shooting is similar to passing. The difference is when it is used. Have your players stand directly over the ball. They must be balanced. They have to lift their kicking leg so the knee of that leg is pointing downward toward the ball and the foot is up and behind them.

2. The leg that is not being used to kick the ball will be planted beside it. The toe of the plant foot must be pointed in the direction the shot is intended to go because when the ball is kicked, the direction the plant foot is pointing is the direction the ball will travel.

3. The ankle of the foot kicking the ball must be locked into place. This is true every time the ball is struck.

4. Players must look up at where they want to shoot, and then back at the ball so their eyes are on the ball at the time of the shot.

   As the kicking foot swings toward the ball, the toe of that foot needs to be locked and pointing straight down and slightly to the right of the ball, if kicking with the right foot, or down and pointing slightly to the left of the ball, if using the left foot. This type of kick gives the player more strength in the kick. If using the instep the procedure is the same as with passing.

5. When the foot strikes the ball, the foot and leg must not stop moving. The momentum of the kick should cause the foot to connect with the ball and carry the ball all the way through the kick. Never stop the straight motion of the kick when the ball is hit with the foot, as it is important for the foot to follow through all the way to the finish position.

6. When your players shoot on goal they need to do it quickly. Stopping the ball and then backing up before shooting, or moving the ball right or left and delaying the shot in any way, allows the defender to get to the ball or the goalkeeper to get into position, making it more difficult to score.

7. Player balance is important when shooting. Balance allows power and accuracy. However, if your player has an open shot and is off balance, he or she needs to take the shot anyway.

8. When shooting the ball on goal, the ball must be kicked away from the goalkeeper. Your players will see the goalkeeper and concentrate on him or her, but practice with them to make sure they shoot away from the goalkeeper to an open space inside the goal, not directly at the goalkeeper.

9. Accuracy is the most important aspect of shooting. The position in which your player is standing determines the strength

needed on the shot. If your player is close to the goal, he or she can easily pass the ball into the goal. If your player is a distance away from the goal, however, a harder shot is required to get the speed necessary to beat the goalkeeper.

10. The normal shot on goal will be hard. Have players put all of their weight and strength behind the kick by leaning forward when shooting. Their kicking leg should follow all the way through the ball as well.

11. After your player shoots, he or she needs to move forward to follow the ball. This is done in case the ball bounces off the goalkeeper, a defender, or the goal post. This will enable your player to get a second shot off the rebound.

NOTE: As you work with your players, remind them that when shooting the ball on goal they must always kick away from the goalkeeper. This must be taught early and often. A good way to teach this is to place a few cones at the right and left corners of the goal and have your player try to knock down the cones when they shoot. Don't just have them kick the ball at the goal. They must learn to accurately place the ball. Remember, you can buy small portable soccer goals or you may use cones to set the right and left parameters of the goal. This then becomes the goal. Young soccer players tend to look at the goal, see the goalkeeper, and kick to that person. The goalkeeper is a no-kick area, and all kicks must be to the right or left of him or her.

Distance Kick (B)

What Is Needed: Each player has a ball, and cones are used to mark the starting and stopping points.

How to Do It: Line all of your players up so they are in a straight line. If you are practicing on a playing field, line them up on one touchline as the start and use the other touchline as the end. If you are on an open field, use cones for the start and stop.

This drill is done two different ways. The first is to have your players step back from the ball one step. At the sound of the whistle, all players take one step to the ball and kick it as hard as they can. They then run to the ball again and stop one step from the ball. Repeat this action until everyone's ball rolls across the stop line. Run this drill back and forth using the right foot for one direction and the left foot for the other direction. Make sure they all know who finished first, but congratulate everyone, even the weaker kickers as they, too, will develop over time.

Once the players are kicking the ball correctly, have them start three steps back from the ball, run to the ball, plant their foot, and kick. They will continue kicking while they run, all the way across the field. Again, use the opposite foot coming back. The object of this drill is to learn to kick properly, get a cardio-vascular workout, and build shooting strength with both feet.

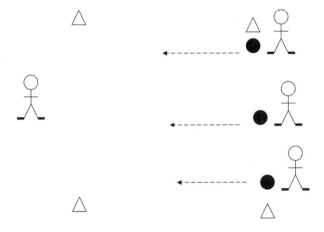

Figure 13.14. Distance Kick

Animal Kick (B)

What You Need: Every player needs a ball. Enough cones to set up a goal.

How to Do It: Set up the cones to form a goal and then move the players so they are lined up side by side facing it, but at least fifteen feet away. Ask each player to pick an animal they want to imitate. Kids will usually pick animals like horses, dogs, and cats, but they can pick any that makes a noise.

Let the first player take off dribbling toward the goal. While dribbling, he or she has to make an animal sound. Players will do this from the time they start until they shoot the ball into the goal and score.

As soon as the first player is halfway to the goal, start the next player. Have the returning player go back and get ready to go again. On the next time through, the players can pick a new animal or stay with their previous choice.

The object of this drill is to improve dribbling skills and to help the players learn to shoot while on the run.

Foot Throw (I)

This drill is good to do when your players are at rest. This can be done with or without help from another player. It will be a little bit difficult at first, but your players will easily pick it up. The object is to throw or pass the ball to another player using only one's feet. When you tell your players to throw you the ball, always make them use their feet.

What You Need: Give each player a ball.

How to Do It:
1. Place the ball in front of your player, within reach of his or her foot.
2. Have your players place the soles of their shoes on top of the ball. Then, applying pressure to the ball, have them roll their feet backward while keeping contact with the ball. This causes the ball to roll backward toward your players.

3. Once the ball is moving backward, have them quickly place the foot they just used to roll the ball on the ground directly in front of the ball. The toe of the shoe has to be on the ground and the heel of the shoe slightly elevated.
4. Position the foot so the ball can roll up on the top of the shoe.
5. When the ball rolls up on the shoe, have your players kick foot and leg forward to throw the ball away from them. Be sure to tell them to keep their ankle locked.

Another way to do this is to have them throw the ball to you using their foot as the ball rolls to them. Pass the ball to the players and have them let the ball roll up on their foot. They lift their foot and return the ball using the same technique they used originally to throw it. This is harder to do, and they will need to master the standing throw first.

Place Foot on   Pull Foot Back   Let the Ball Roll   Pass Ball
Top of Ball   to Roll Ball   Upon the Foot

Figure 13.15. Foot Throw

Spot Ball (I)
What You Need: This requires all players, multiple balls, a goal, cones, and a goalkeeper.

How to Do It: This drill teaches your players to shoot on the goal at different distances and angles, develop a sense of goal location, and use both feet. The object of this drill is to perform stationary kicks at different distances and angles.

This drill is multifaceted and can be used many different ways.

Place about three to five cones around the face of the goal. Make sure they are at different distances and different angles to the goal. Have your players place a ball next to the cone, one ball on each side. The player kicking the ball on the left side of the cone uses the right foot, and the player kicking the ball on the right side of the cone uses the left foot. Have the players start with one step and kick. Have the players alternate the side they kick from each time.

With the ball stationary, have your players take a one-step approach to the ball, make the kick, and follow it up. Put constant emphasis on the importance of kicking the ball away from the goalkeeper.

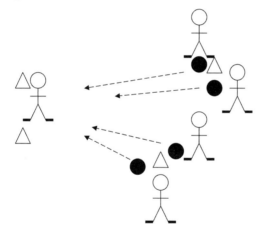

Figure 13.16. Spot Ball

A variation on this drill is to place multiple balls on each side and have one player from each side run to the ball, kick, and then move to the next. They must keep moving, only stopping when they actually kick.

This drill can also be used for two teams. The object is to see which team can score the most goals. Set up cones and place the ball on one side only. Have each player on the kicking team kick the ball. The team that is not kicking gathers the balls and rolls them back to the kicking team. After each person on one team has kicked, the teams swap positions. Have each team kick with both the right and left foot before you announce the winner. Count the balls out loud as they go into the goal. Do not stop the balls from going into the goal.

Go to the Ball and Kick (I)

What You Need: Set up two cones to make a goal or use a small-side goal. This is done with one player and one ball at a time.

How to Do It: This drill teaches your player how to focus on the ball, move to the ball, dribble, and shoot. Have your player stand facing the goal with his or her back to you. All players need to be together. You will serve as the ball thrower. When you throw the ball, call out a name and let that player move to the ball. Immediately after the first person goes after the ball, throw the second ball. Standing behind your player, throw the ball over his or her head so it goes toward the direction of the goal.

When your players see the ball come over their head and hear their name, they will then run to the ball and pass it into the goal.

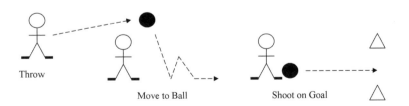

Throw   Move to Ball   Shoot on Goal

Figure 13.17. Go to the Ball and Kick

Make sure they pass using their instep, top of foot, and outside of foot. The object of this drill is to help them to focus on the ball quickly, move to it, and pass the ball into the goal.

You can change the game by having your players face you, with their backs to the goal, while you throw it over their head, making them turn and run to the ball. You can also throw it to their side or between their legs. Give them as many different combinations as you can. Once they start to improve, move back and have them dribble to the goal before they shoot.

Moving Shot (I)

What You Need: This drill has the same requirements as the last.

How to Do It: The moving shot teaches your players to shoot on the move and develop a sense of goal location. It requires them to shoot quickly, shoot with accuracy, and use both feet. Keep the cones in the same location as in the drill above, but have your player move approximately four or five yards away from the cones. Have them dribble the soccer ball to the cone and shoot when they reach it. This requires them to concentrate on the dribble, look at the goal, and shoot to the open part of the goal.

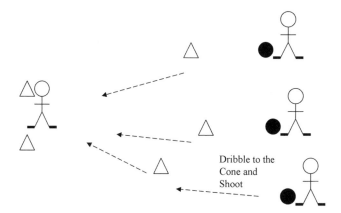

Dribble to the Cone and Shoot

Figure 13.18. Moving Shot

Turn and Shoot (A)

What You Need: One ball, numerous cones, players, a goal, and a goalkeeper.

How to Do It: This drill teaches your players to move to open space to shoot quickly. Have each player move away from the goal and the cones. Have them start to dribble across the face of the goal. Yell to them to turn. They turn toward the goal and shoot when they are ready. To make this happen, have your player find an open space between the cones to shoot on goal. They must shoot as soon as they are open and not wait.

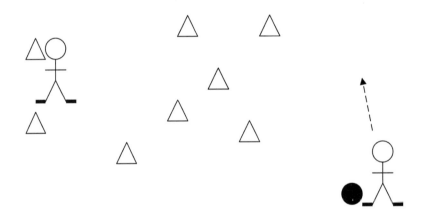

Figure 13.19. Turn and Shoot

Pass, Receive, and Shoot (A)

What You Need: This requires all players, one ball, a goal, numerous cones, and a goalkeeper.

How to Do It: This drill teaches your player to choose the appropriate foot, shoot on the run, and shoot accurately. Have your players move away from the goal and then have them run toward the goal. As they are approaching the goal, pass the ball to them and have them shoot.

Start with one touch, or shooting as the ball reaches them, and then add cones and have them receive the ball, move to an open space, and shoot. The passes can be done from numerous locations to help them learn to shoot a ball coming toward them, as it is centered, and from behind them.

Place players on each side and use the assistant coach to pass on the other side. After the player has kicked using one foot, have them move to the other side so they can kick with the other foot. This keeps the drill moving and lets each player kick with both feet.

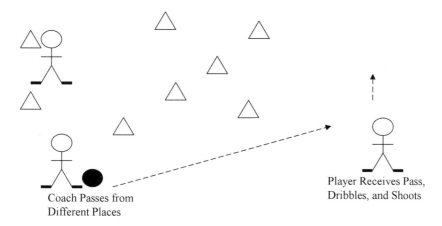

Coach Passes from Different Places

Player Receives Pass, Dribbles, and Shoots

Figure 13.20. Pass, Receive, and Shoot

Combination Pass and Shoot (A)

What You Need: This requires two players, a ball, a goal, and numerous cones.

How to Do It: This drill reinforces dribbling, passing, and goal techniques and teaches shot timing. The object of this drill is to teach your players to move toward the goal by dribbling and passing and then to move to an open space so they can shoot on goal.

Move your players away from the goal. Have the players spread out but stay even with each other. The player with the ball dribbles and then passes the ball to the other player. After the pass, the player moves to an open space, and the other player passes back to them. The player receiving the ball then shoots on goal. Use a goalkeeper.

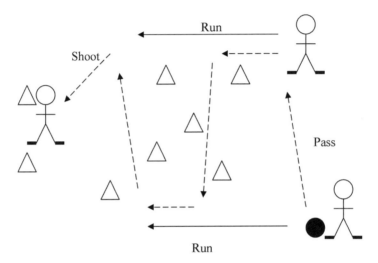

Figure 13.21. Combination Pass and Shoot

Kick Ball and One Touch Shot (A)
What You Need: This requires players, one ball, a goal, numerous cones, and a goalkeeper.
How to Do It: This drill is to teach your players to control the ball, use the appropriate foot, do a one touch shot on the run, and shoot accurately.

Have your players move away from the goal and then have them run toward it. As they are approaching the goal, dropkick the ball to them so it is bouncing as they reach it. They must go to the ball, control it, and then shoot on goal. Start with one touch, shooting as the ball reaches them, and then have them receive the ball and move to an open space to shoot. The passes can be done from numerous locations to help them learn to shoot a ball coming toward them, as it is centered, and from behind them.

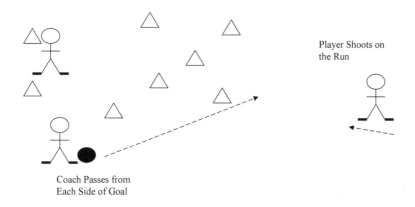

Figure 13.22. Kick Ball and One Touch Shot

Pass and Go (A)

What You Need: This drill uses you, one player at a time, one ball, and cones to serve as defenders.

How to Do It: The concept behind this drill is to teach your players to dribble, judge distance, pass, defend, and touch on the ball. You will be the center person of this drill. Your player will be the person executing the play. The official name of this action is a wall pass. Your player will dribble, pass, and receive the ball. Both of you are offensive players.

Give your player the ball and have him or her stand facing you, but off to the side, about three to five yards away. Place a cone in the center of the drill area to represent a defender. Have your player dribble the ball until he or she is about five feet from the defender (cone) and then pass the ball to you.

When your player passes the ball to you, you will deflect the ball behind the defender (cone).

Make sure your player passes to you using the instep, top of foot, and outside of foot. Your player will then move to the side of the cone opposite from you, retrieve the ball, and continue on.

If you have an assistant coach, this person can be placed on the other side of the cone so your player can pass to either side. If you don't have another person, move from side to side so your players can learn to use both feet from both directions.

After your players understand the concept and get good at the drill, replace the cone with an actual defensive player.

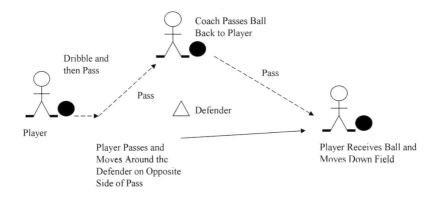

Figure 13.23. Pass and Go

THROW-IN

Why?

When the ball rolls out of the field of play by going over the touchline, it must be put back in play by throwing the ball onto the field. There is a designated way to do this and it is referred to as a throw-in. Proper technique and accuracy is a must for a throw-in.

Basic: Throwing the ball into the field of play while standing flat-footed. Ages 4 and 5.

Intermediate: Throwing the ball into the field of play directly to a teammate while the thrower is standing still. Age 6.

Advanced: Throwing the ball to a teammate's head, chest, or feet while moving to the line for the throw. Ages 7 and 8.

How?

1. To start with, the rules of the game require that your players keep a part of both feet on the ground as they throw the ball. If either foot leaves the ground, it is an infraction of the rules, and the ball is turned over to the other team to throw-in. In U-6 play, however, the player will get a second chance to throw the ball in properly.

2. When the ball is thrown into the field of play, it must be thrown so it goes directly over the head and moves and spins forward without the ball spinning to the right or the left. The ball should spin in the direction of the throw, top over bottom.

3. Both hands must be used on a throw-in. The easiest way is to grip the ball with both hands, one on each side of the ball. The thumbs should be on the back of the ball and touching with the fingers on the sides of the ball. Ideally, your players' hands will form a "W" on the back of the ball.

4. To get better distance, your players need to move the ball back so it is over and behind their head. They need to extend their arms as far back as they can. Also have your players lean back as far as they can while still maintaining their balance.

5. Have your players throw the ball forward onto the field using both arms and bending their body so it moves with the movement and direction of the throw. Older players can move a few steps back from the touchline, then move quickly to the line and throw using their forward momentum. The player will have to plant their front foot and drag the back toe to maintain contact with the ground.

6. The ball should be thrown directly to a teammate and can be thrown so it lands exactly where your player wants it to. It can be higher in the air if it is to be used for heading the ball or thrown low so the receiving teammate can use his or her feet to trap or kick the ball. As soon as the ball is thrown in, the player that threw the ball must get back on the field to continue play or to potentially receive a pass back from the receiver.

Ball Throw (B)

What You Need: This drill uses sets of two players, each set with one ball.

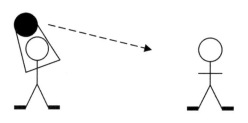

Figure 13.24. Ball Throw

How to Do It: This drill teaches your player the proper technique for a basic throw-in. Your players line up in sets of two with each set facing each other about six feet apart. You can adjust them as you see the distance of their throws. Walk up and down the line of players watching each player carefully to make sure they are executing the throw-in properly. As your players begin to throw better, increase the distance between them and continue the drill. Most younger players cannot catch the ball, so tell them to let the thrown ball fall to the ground and have them pick it up to throw it back.

Throw to Cones (B)

What You Need: This drill uses one ball for each player.

How to Do It: This drill teaches your players the proper technique and the accuracy needed for a throw-in. Place your players in a circle with the cones in the middle. Have them throw at the cones that are laid out in front of them. Their goal is to hit the cones with the ball. Have them repeat the throws until they are able to place the ball with accuracy while using proper technique. Have your players grab the ball closest to them rather than chasing after their own ball. This saves time. As your players begin to throw better, increase the distance between them and continue the drill.

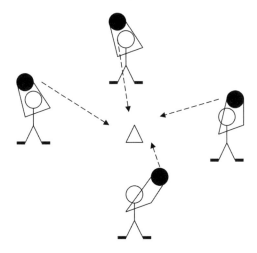

Figure 13.25. Throw to Cones

Dodge Ball (I)

What You Need: This drill uses all players with their own ball, plus the assistant coach.

How to Do It: This drill teaches your players how to throw for distance and accuracy to a moving target. Mark out an area where your throwing players will stand. Then have the assistant coach stand about five to ten feet away from the players. Have the players throw the ball directly to the assistant coach. The assistant coach will dodge the ball.

After the throw the players gather their own balls and repeat the drill. If anyone actually hits the coach, congratulate them and make a big deal over it. This will make the others try harder. The throws will not be hard, so the assistant coach will not be hurt. You must watch the players as they throw to ensure their technique is correct. As you continue the drill, gradually increase the distance so the thrower has to learn to gauge the strength of the throw and develop accuracy.

These are young players, so if there is a near miss or a hit, have your assistant play along and fall down and roll over, or anything to make it more fun.

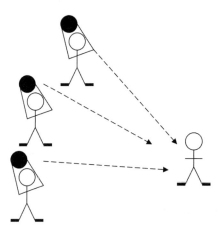

Figure 13.26. Dodge Ball

Moving Throw (A)

What You Need: This drill uses numerous balls and all of your players, with one player performing the throw-in and the other players ready to receive the ball or to take away the ball.

How to Do It: Place one player behind the touchline to execute the throw-in. Split the other players into two teams. One team, designated the offense, receives the ball, and the other, designated the defense, takes away the ball from the offensive players attempting to receive it. Start by having the offensive players run parallel to the touchline and have the thrower throw the ball at the feet of one of those players. Repeat the drill by having the players move from out in the field toward the touchline, with the thrower throwing the ball to each player's chest, or by having them move out in the field to head the ball on the throw-in. Repeat running both left and right. Also practice throwing down the touchline toward your goal and to another player.

This drill can be done standing still or by moving toward the line and then throwing.

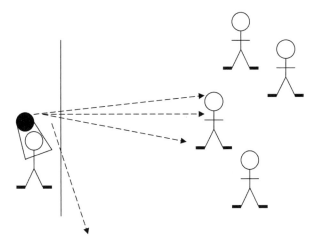

Figure 13.27. Moving Throw

TRAPPING AND RECEIVING

Why?
When one teammate passes the ball to another, the receiver must be able to stop the ball and gain control of it. It is similar to

catching a ball with one's hands, except in this case the player must catch the soccer ball with his or her feet or body. Your players must be able to stop the ball and still maintain control of it, not allowing it bounce away. Catching the ball is called receiving. Stopping the ball is called trapping. Your player must be able to receive the ball with his or her head, chest, thigh, or feet.

Basic: Stop the movement of the ball using the feet. Ages 4, 5, and 6.

Intermediate: Stop the ball by receiving it with the foot or by trapping it with the foot. Age 7.

Advanced: Gain control of the ball by receiving with all parts of the body and by trapping the ball. Age 8.

How?

1. When the ball is kicked by a teammate or an opponent, your players need to move so they are in the direct path of the ball. This will center their body on the ball. They should not wait for the ball to reach them, but move towards the ball to receive it.

2. When the ball reaches your players, have them extend their foot out to contact the ball. As the ball reaches the foot, your players must gently place their foot against the ball while at the same time moving it in the direction the ball is moving so they can ease the ball to a stop or a near stop and gain control of it. This is done by allowing the ball to move with the movement of your player's foot. If your player just sticks out a foot, the ball will hit it and bounce away, out of control.

3. To trap or stop the ball, simply have your players step on the top of the ball with the sole of their shoe to stop its rolling motion. This takes timing, but your players will be able to develop the skill with practice.

4. Once your player has control of the ball, either by trapping or by receiving, he or she needs to be able to dribble away from the other players, or pass the ball to another teammate.

Pass and Receive (B)

What You Need: This drill uses two players and one ball.

How to Do It: This drill teaches your players to pass and receive the ball. U-6 players should only concentrate on using their feet to receive the ball. The portions below that incorporate the use of other parts of the body and are for U-8 players and above.

Kick to Feet

Figure 13.28. Pass and Receive

The object of this drill is to teach your players how to receive the ball using their feet. Start by having one player pass the ball to the feet of the other player. Remember, the players must meet the ball with their foot and then withdraw it quickly to stop its momentum.

Trap the Ball (B)

What You Need: This drill uses two players and one ball.

How to Do It: This drill teaches your players to trap the ball with their feet. Have one player pass the ball, again on the ground, but this time have the receiving player lift his or her leg and then place a foot on top of the ball to stop it. This takes timing and will be difficult at first but will become easier with practice.

Next, have one player throw the ball to the other player, with the ball bouncing along the ground. As the ball is bouncing, have the receiving player move towards the ball, place a foot on top of it, and step down to stop its movement.

It is important to time the placing of the foot on the ball. Your players will need to do it just as the ball touches the ground from the bounce. The ball should stop completely with no bounce after their foot has been placed on the ball. This takes timing and coordination, but it will develop with time and practice.

Throw Overhand
or Underhand and
Trap with Foot

Kick to Foot
and Trap

Figure 13.29. Trap the Ball

Move and Receive or Trap (I)

What You Need: This drill uses two players and one ball.

How to Do It: This drill teaches your player to trap/receive the ball using the proper technique. The object of this drill is to further enhance receiving and trapping skills and should be practiced with some distance between you and your players.

Player

Player

Receive or Trap

Kick, Throw, or Pass

Figure 13.30. Move and Receive or Trap

Place your players approximately three to five yards apart, and using the same receiving and trapping skills practiced above, have one of the players throw or pass the ball. Make sure the player receiving the ball moves toward it, squares him- or herself to it, and uses the appropriate technique to trap it. Your player will have to determine the proper technique to use.

Body (A)

What You Need: This drill uses two players and one ball, one player throwing the ball and the other player receiving the ball.

How to Do It: Position your two players so they are facing each other. Have one throw the ball while the other player moves to position themselves in front of it. Start by having the player receive the ball with his or her head. This is done by moving the head back as the ball makes contact, to take the momentum off the ball so it falls to the ground in front of the player. Next have them throw to the chest. The movement is always the same. The player must meet and withdraw with the contact of the ball to

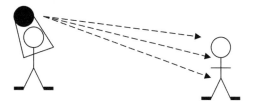

Figure 13.31. Body

stop its movement and let it drop to the feet. The next throw is to the thigh, which is done the same way.

After the player has received the ball three or four times using each method, switch the players so the thrower is now receiving the ball. Walk among your players and observe them to ensure they are using the proper technique.

Receive or Trap and Shoot (A)

What You Need: This drill uses two or three players and one ball. To make this a game situation you can place a goalkeeper in the goal. If you have another player available, you can move him or her between the two players as a defender.

How to Do It: This drill teaches your players trapping, receiving, offense, dribbling, and shooting using the proper techniques. The object of this drill is to continue to work on trapping and receiving techniques and to add dribbling and shooting. A goalkeeper and defender can be added to make this more difficult and to replicate what your players will see in a game.

Kick or throw the ball to the player, then have them stop the ball and dribble toward the goal to shoot. If you have a goalkeeper, ensure that your players shoot away from him or her. Make sure your players do not use their head or chest if the ball is kicked high in the air and has not touched the ground first.

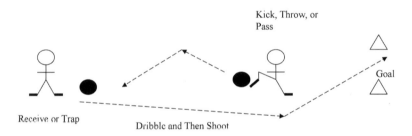

Figure 13.32. Receive or Trap and Shoot

SHIELDING

Why?

Shielding the ball is a method used to keep the ball away from an opponent while dribbling or looking to pass the ball to a teammate. The act of shielding is done by putting one's body between the ball and the opponent.

Basic: Turn one's back to the opposing player and dribble away or pass the ball to a teammate. Age 6.

Intermediate: Place one's body between the ball and the opposing player while maintaining control of the ball, either to dribble to open space or to pass to a teammate. Age 7.

Advanced: Place one's body between the ball and the opposing player while maintaining control of the ball; move the ball with one's feet to keep the opposing player away from it. The next step is to pass the ball to a teammate as quickly as one can. Age 8.

How?

1. When your players are approached by a defender, have them turn until their body is between their opponent and the ball.
2. With the ball on the other side of the opponent, have your player dribble away from the opponent or look for a teammate to pass to.
3. When shielding the ball to keep it away from the opponent, make sure your player always uses proper dribbling techniques. Tell your player to keep the ball close to themselves to maintain control.

Numerous Moves (B)

What You Need: A ball for each player and numerous cones.

How to Do It: This drill teaches your player touch on the ball and ball control. Set up the cones so they are at different locations around the field. Have your players dribble while moving around the cones. They can use any technique they want, whether it's using their instep to move the ball sideways, the sole of their shoe rolled across the top of the ball to move it in any direction, or moving it with the outside of their foot. Each technique moves the ball in a different direction.

Figure 13.33. Numerous Moves

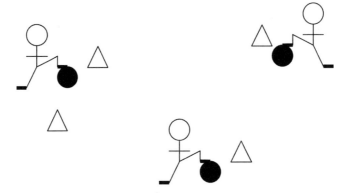

Shield and Move (I)

What You Need: This drill uses teams of two players with one ball per team and cones to mark out an area.

How to Do It: This drill teaches your players to shield the ball, control it, and be aware of the opposition. Give one player from each team a ball and have him or her dribble it. The other player will act as a defender and try to take the ball away from the dribbler.

Figure 13.34. Shield and Move

As the dribblers are approached by the defenders, have them put their body between the defender and the ball. Have the players dribble away from the defenders as soon as they can. Tell your defensive player not to bump or push the dribbler in an effort to get to the ball.

Shield and Move, and Shield, Move, and Pass (A)

What You Need: This drill uses two players, one ball, and cones to mark out an area. All players can do this drill at the same time, but they must work in teams of two. Each pair consists of one offensive player with a ball and one defensive player trying to get the ball.

How to Do It: This drill is to teach your players to shield, offense, defense, pass, and dribble. This is similar to the above drill but adds passing/shooting of the ball.

Use cones to mark the outside boundaries of the practice area but place cones inside and outside the area. Have your players dribble around the inside area, avoiding the cones while keeping the ball away from the other player.

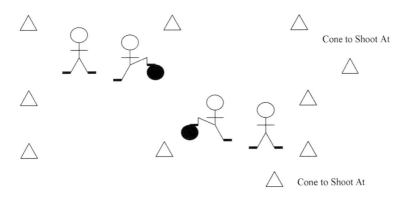

Figure 13.35. Shield, Move, and Pass

When the player is able to get open, tell them to shoot or pass the ball to an outside cone. During this drill the defensive player can gently push or bump the player with the ball. Let them know that this will happen during the game. Also let them know that it is part of the game and to play on. If it is bad, the referee will call a penalty.

HEADING

Why?

Heading the ball is using your head to strike the ball and redirect it while it's in the air. If it is done correctly, it will not hurt your player. They must use their forehead. Not the top of their head, their face, or their temples. Heading the ball can enable your player to pass the ball to another player or even shoot on goal.

> *NOTE:* When you first start working with your players on this drill, take one of the balls and deflate it until it is soft. This way they can get used to using their forehead and not get hurt if it hits their nose, etc.

Basic: Learn the proper technique used to head the ball. Age 6.
Intermediate: Head the ball directly back to the thrower. Age 7.
Advanced: Head the ball in any direction with accuracy. Age 8.

How?

1. When the soccer ball is coming toward them, make sure that your players move into the direct path of the ball. Emphasize to your players that they need to square their body to the ball. They must do this every time they attempt to head the ball.

2. As the ball is coming towards your players, have them watch the ball closely. While they are watching the ball, they need to move into the direct path of the ball so it will strike them in the center of their forehead.

3. To head or redirect the ball up into the air, the player must strike the bottom half of the ball. To head the ball toward the ground the player must strike the ball on the top half of the ball.

4. Your player cannot close their eyes as the ball comes to them. They need to continue to watch the ball as it contacts their forehead.

5. Tell you players to keep their eyes open so they can see the ball coming toward them, hitting their head, and then moving away from them. Closing their eyes can cause them to move their head and the ball can end up hitting someplace other than the forehead. This may cause them to get hurt.

6. The proper movement for heading the ball is to have your player move their head backward as the ball is coming toward them. As the ball nears them, have them snap their head forward so their head is still moving forward when the ball reaches them. They will move their head into the ball, striking it. If your player stands still and lets the ball hit them, it will hurt. Snapping their head forward to strike the ball will hurt less and will also put more force behind the strike.

The drills below teach the proper movement of the head and should be done before moving on to the more advanced drills. Remember to start with a ball that is slightly deflated, making it softer.

Proper Movement (B)
What You Need: This drill uses you, all of your players and slightly deflated balls.

How to Do It: This drill teaches your players proper motion and use of the head to strike the ball.

Start by having your players sit on the ground with their feet straight out in front of them. Move so you are standing in front of your player. Throw the deflated ball underhanded toward your player's head. Throw the ball so it falls short of the head. This requires your player to lean forward with the upper body to strike the soccer ball with the forehead.

This establishes the motion your player will always use when heading the ball. Move from one player to another as you go down the line. As with most drills, if you have an assistant coach, you can split the players into two groups to accomplish more is a shorter period of time.

Once the players are doing well using their forehead and back and forth motion, have your players repeat the drill from a kneeling position. Again, make your underhanded throw fall short of your players. They can head the ball back to you and then fall forward, landing on their hands. Don't throw so short that they have to lunge to get the ball.

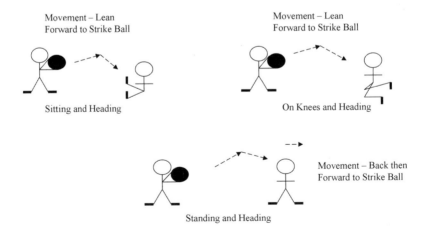

Movement – Lean Forward to Strike Ball

Sitting and Heading

Movement – Lean Forward to Strike Ball

On Knees and Heading

Standing and Heading

Movement – Back then Forward to Strike Ball

Figure 13.36. Proper Movement

The final step is to have them stand up and use the same technique they used while sitting and kneeling.

Throw and Head (I)

What You Need: This drill uses two players working as a team. Only one ball is required.

How to Do It: This drill teaches your players proper head motion, skill, and accuracy when using the head to redirect the ball. The object of this drill is to again work on the heading technique but to have your player move to where the ball is thrown. Have your players hold a ball in their hands and then throw the ball into the air. Make sure they move to the ball and using the back and forth motion, head the ball to the other player. You can vary this drill by having them throw the ball in the air and head to a goal or another object to work on accuracy.

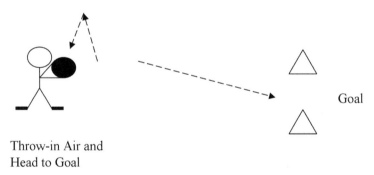

Throw-in Air and
Head to Goal

Goal

Figure 13.37. Throw and Head

Change Direction (A)

What You Need: This drill uses two players and one ball.

How to Do It: This drill teaches your players how to properly head the soccer ball to redirect it to a teammate or open space. Have each player stand facing another. Have one player throw the ball underhanded to the other player. Have the players that are going to head the ball stand so their body is facing the person throwing the ball. Their feet will be planted, and they will watch the ball coming to them.

Instead of just heading the ball back to the thrower, the players should turn the entire upper portion of their body so that they are able to strike the ball by coming at it from a side angle. This causes the ball to change direction. Make sure your player uses the proper motion by leaning backwards and striking the ball while snapping the head forward.

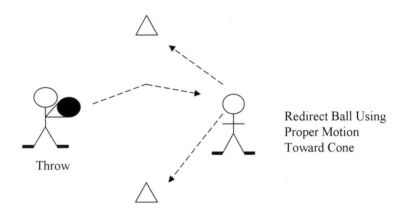

Figure 13.38. Change Direction

Head on Goal (A)

What You Need: This drill uses each player and you. Only one ball is required, but numerous balls can be used.

How to Do It: This drill teaches your players how to redirect the ball with accuracy, how to move and adjust to the ball, and to head the ball while on the move.

Set up some cones for the goal and then have your player move about three to five yards directly in front it. You will move to the side of the goal so you are directly even with your player.

Again you will be about three to five yards away from your player. Throw the ball into the air and have your player move to the ball and head the ball toward the goal.

When your players are doing well, increase the difficulty by having them move to the opposite side of the field and run straight at you as you throw the ball. When they run in, have them stop, get set, and then head the ball.

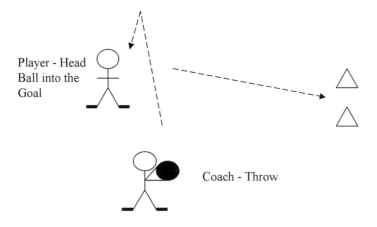

Figure 13.39. Head on Goal

Heading While Running (A)
What You Need: This drill uses each player and you. Only one ball is required, but numerous balls can be used.

How to Do It: This drill teaches your players to head in a game-type situation. It also emphasizes accuracy, direction, and timing. The object of this drill is to teach your player to head while running. It also allows them to head the ball goal against a goalkeeper.

Place your player approximately five or more yards from the goal, centered on the goal, and facing it. You will stand to the right or left of the goal. Have your players start running toward the goal, and while they are running, you will throw the ball into the air. The throw can be directly in their running path, or to the right or left of the players.

Throwing the soccer ball right or left causes your players to adjust their run and reposition themselves in order to head it. Make sure they head the ball on the goal, but away from the goalkeeper.

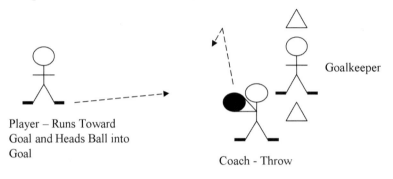

Player – Runs Toward Goal and Heads Ball into Goal

Goalkeeper

Coach - Throw

Figure 13.40. Heading While Running

JUGGLING

Why?

Juggling is one of the best ways your players can learn proper touch on the ball. The object is to keep the ball in the air, constantly moving, using different parts of the body. It is a way to play with the ball and have fun while learning how the ball will react to different touches. Your players can do this by themselves or with friends and teammates.

Basic: Bounce or juggle the ball using the feet, knees, and head. Age 6.

Intermediate: Juggle the ball using the feet, knees, and head with accuracy and control. Age 7.

Advanced: Juggle using the feet, knees, and head between multiple players. Age 8.

How?

1. Any time the ball is being juggled, make sure your players watch the ball closely. Taking their eyes off the ball as it approaches them will result in a poor touch on the ball.
2. There are no set rules. Your players can juggle the ball with their feet, knees, or head. Any part of the body that can be used to control the ball is okay, with the exception of the hands and arms.
3. Watch your players as they juggle and make sure they use different parts of their body to juggle. Don't let them use just one foot or just their knees. Make them use their feet, knees, and head. Their skill will improve much faster if they do.
4. If your players are using their feet to juggle, they can use the top of their shoe. They can also use their instep when their proficiency advances.
5. Make sure your players strike the ball while they are balanced. The ball needs to move straight up and straight down. Do not over-kick the soccer ball. Gentle and controlled touches are best.

Feet and Knee Juggling (B)

What You Need: This drill uses one player and one ball.

How to Do It: The object of this drill is to teach your player ball control and touch on the ball. Learning to juggle properly must be done in individual steps. When your players are just beginning to juggle, ask them to use one foot only. When your players have mastered bouncing the ball on that foot, have them switch to the other foot. When they can do it with each foot, start them using both feet. Do the same thing with the knees. Once they are using both feet and both knees, have them concentrate on not using the same part of the body two times in a row.

Figure 13.41. Feet and Knee Juggling

Head Juggling (B)

What You Need: This drill uses one player and one ball.

How to Do It: The object of this drill is to teach your players to use their head for ball control and touch on the ball. Have your players throw the ball above them and then move until their forehead is positioned directly beneath the ball. Your players must be balanced under the ball so when it hits their forehead the ball will bounce straight up and down. Have your players bend their knees and move into the ball to propel it. Have them start with short taps to learn to control the ball. They can increase the force of the header as they improve. See how many times they can head the ball before it touches the ground.

Players can also bounce the ball off a fence or wall of the house to learn more control with their head. Once they have learned this drill, incorporate it into the feet and knee juggling drills. Your players will now be juggling with their feet, knees, and head. Using all three body parts, they'll be able to control the ball for many touches. After they have done this for a while, you will also notice your players' skills in the other aspects of soccer improving as well.

Head Only

Figure 13.42. Head Juggling

Through the Cones (I)

What You Need: This drill uses a ball for each player and cones.

How to Do It: This drill teaches your players to move to the ball and control the ball while moving. All of this is done using control and juggling techniques. Set up the cones next to each other and in a straight line. Start the drill by having a player start juggling and then move through the cones. Your player moves with the ball, controlling it through the cones while maintaining the juggle.

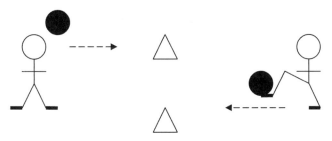

Figure 13.43. Through the Cones

Juggling While Moving (I)

What You Need: This drill uses one player and one ball.

How to Do It: The object of this drill is to teach your player to juggle the ball while moving. Have your player start juggling. Then have him or her start moving around the area while still maintaining control of the ball. Start slow and then pick up the speed as they improve.

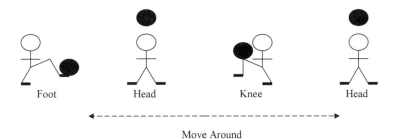

Figure 13.44. Juggling While Moving

Over the Cones (A)

What You Need: Two players, one ball, and cones.

How to Do It: Give one player the ball to juggle. When he or she has control of the ball, it is passed over the cones to the other player who gains control of the ball and juggles until he or she has control and then passes it back. Try to have your players do this without letting the ball ever touch the ground. If they can't, set the number of touches, such as one bounce or two bounces.

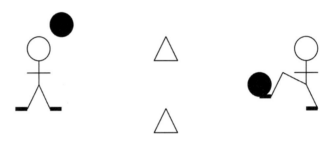

Figure 13.45. Over the Cones

VOLLEY

Why?

A volley kick is a technique used to kick the ball while it is still in the air. This will be a little difficult for your players to learn, but is very effective. The volley can be used when shooting on the goal or by the defense when they need to quickly clear the ball out of their goal area.

Basic: Return the ball using the foot to volley. Age 7.

Intermediate: Move to the ball and use the appropriate volley technique to clear the ball. Age 7.

Advanced: Move to the ball and use the appropriate volley technique to shoot on goal. Age 8.

How?

1. To properly perform a volley kick, your players must move so they are directly in front of the ball with their body squared to it so they can receive it.
2. As the ball approaches your players, make sure they watch the ball very closely.
3. When the ball reaches them, they need to kick it using the same techniques they use in shooting (ankle locked, top of foot, inside of foot).
4. The difference in a volley kick is that your player's knee will be in the air when the ball is hit. The upper portion of the leg will be parallel to the ground. The portion of the leg from the knee to the foot swings forward striking the ball while it is in the air. The toe of the foot will be pointing straight down toward the ground.
5. After players strike the ball, their foot must follow all the way through the kick.

Volley with Top of Foot (B)

What You Need: This drill uses you, the players, and one ball.

How to Do It: This drill teaches your players the proper way to volley the ball using the tops of their feet. Place your player in front of you, approximately six feet away. Make an underhand throw of the ball to them. Your players need to square themselves to the ball, lift their knee, point their toe toward the ground, bring the bottom half of their leg to the rear, and then let their foot swing forward to strike the ball.

Throw   Volley   Throw   Half-Volley

Figure 13.46. Volley with Top of Foot

Have your players bend over the ball as it arrives and then straighten up as they strike it. Be sure they follow through the ball as they kick. A half-volley is when the ball bounces on the ground prior to reaching the player. It may be easier for your players to start with the half volley and then move into the full volley.

Volley with Side of Foot (B)

What You Need: This drill uses you, the players, and one ball.

How to Do It: This drill teaches your players the proper way to volley the ball using the inside of their foot. Place your players in front of you, approximately six to nine feet away. Make an underhand throw of the ball to them. Your players need to square themselves to the ball, turn partially sideways to strike the ball from the side, lift their knee, level their foot so it can strike the ball, bring their leg to the rear, and then let their foot swing forward to strike the ball. Be sure they follow through the ball as they kick.

Throw   Volley   Throw   Half-Volley

Figure 13.47. Volley with Side of Foot

Appropriate Volley (I)

What You Need: This drill uses you, the players, one ball, and cones.

How to Do It: This drill teaches your players to volley at different distances and with different types of volleys. Place cones around the area and have your players move to a different cone after each volley. Throw the ball to your players and have them use the appropriate volley to return the ball to you. It can be a full volley or half volley using the top of the foot, side of the foot, and left or right leg. Let your players decide which to use. Also watch their technique to make sure they are performing the volley correctly.

Figure 13.48. Appropriate Volley

Game Volley (A)

What You Need: This drill uses you, the players, one ball, and cones.

How to Do It: This drill teaches your players to volley on the run and on goal. Move a player back approximately fifteen yards from the goal. Stand to the side of your player and throw the ball in his or her general direction. Have your player move to the ball and use the appropriate volley to shoot on goal. Place a goal-keeper in the goal. Your player must work to shoot away from the goalkeeper.

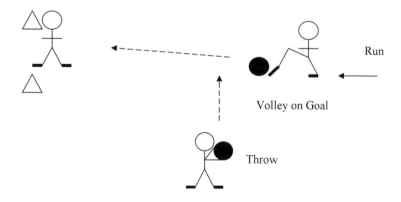

Figure 13.49. Game Volley

GOALKEEPING

This section shows you how to teach your players goalkeeping. The goalkeeper uses skills different than those the field players use. That being said, it is very important that all of the players who learn goalkeeping skills also learn field techniques. Concentrating on just being a goalkeeper can set a player back if they switch to the field. As they get older, they will be more likely to settle on a position, but younger players need to do it all.

Why?

Goalkeepers must be able to catch the ball, kick the ball, and throw the ball. They must also be able to direct other players on the field. Goalkeepers cannot be afraid of the ball, because they must be able to step in front of it and stop it, no matter how fast it is coming. The goalkeeper is a very important part of the team and teams with good goalkeepers tend to win more games than teams with less-skilled ones.

   Basic: Learn the proper position of the hands, arms, and body to receive the ball. Age 7 and 8.
   Intermediate: Receive the ball and clear the ball. Age 7 and 8.
   Advanced: Field the ball from players shooting or heading the ball. Age 7 and 8.

How?

1. A goalkeeper must have good balance and as a result must work on maintaining the correct stance, which is feet at shoulder width, balanced on the ground and pointing slightly outward. The goalkeeper's legs and back should be slightly bent. Arms should be extended out and away from the body to catch the ball or otherwise stop the ball from going into the goal.
2. The goalkeeper must watch the ball and move back and forth in front of the goal as the ball moves around the field. This is to ensure he or she is in the best position to stop the ball.

3. Besides being in the correct position, the goalkeeper must also use proper technique when attempting to stop or catch the ball. Not only does the goalkeeper use his or her arms and hands but the body is sometimes used as a secondary means of stopping the ball.

4. Catching the ball is done with a basic "W" position of the hands.

5. Going down to the ground or diving to stop a ball is not recommended for goalkeepers at this age because a goalkeeper cannot move well if he or she is lying on the ground. If the goalkeeper misses the ball when diving, he or she will be unable to reach it again. There may occur a situation in a game where diving is necessary, but this should be done only as a last resort.

6. The key to a goalkeeper blocking the goal is to reduce the angle of the opponent's shot. The next three graphics are examples of how the proper positioning can reduce the area an opponent has to shoot.

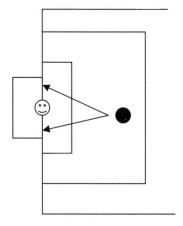

If the Goalkeeper is standing inside the goal or on the goal line, this creates open space on the right and left side of the goal that is out of reach of the goalkeeper.

Figure 13.50 (1). Moving Out of the Goal

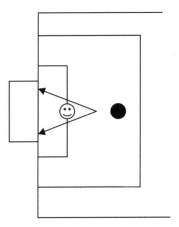

If the Goalkeeper moves outside of the goal, toward the ball and the opposing player, this decreases the open space on the right and left of the goal.

Figure 13.50 (2). Moving Out of the Goal

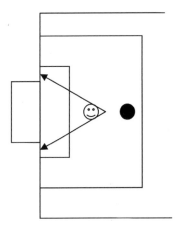

If the Goalkeeper moves farther out of the goal toward the ball and the opposing player this eliminates all open space on the right and left side of the goal. This causes the opposing player to shoot around the goalkeeper, shooting wide of the goal.

Figure 13.50 (3). Moving Out of the Goal

Hand Positions (B)

What You Need: This drill uses you, your goalkeeper, and one ball.

How to Do It: This teaches the proper position of the hands when catching the ball. If the ball is coming to your player and is high, the goalkeeper's hands should be in a "W" position. That means the fingers pointed up and the thumbs pointing in toward each other. If the ball is coming to your player and is below the waist, the hand position will be different. They will be in the "M" position. The palms will be out, fingers pointing down, and thumbs pointing to the right and left of the body. Throw the ball to your goalkeeper, above and below the waist, and make sure he or she uses proper had position when catching it.

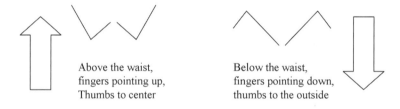

Above the waist,
fingers pointing up,
Thumbs to center

Below the waist,
fingers pointing down,
thumbs to the outside

Figure 13.51. Hand Positions

Body Position (B)

What You Need: This drill uses you, your goalkeeper, and one ball.

How to Do It: This teaches the proper position of the body when scooping the ball. Put your player in front of you and roll the ball to your goalkeeper. Make sure arms are held slightly apart, with palms out and fingers touching the ground, allowing the ball to roll up the arms. As the ball rolls up his or her arms, the goalkeeper must lift them to bring the ball to the chest to hold it and not let it bounce away. When your goalkeeper goes down for the ball make sure his or her legs are positioned so that they will block the ball if it gets past the hands.

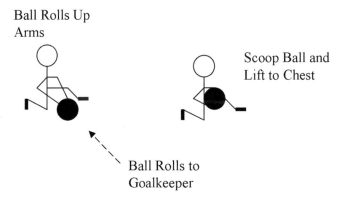

Ball Rolls Up
Arms

Scoop Ball and
Lift to Chest

Ball Rolls to
Goalkeeper

Figure 13.52. Body Position

Overhead Catch (B)

What You Need: This drill uses you, your goalkeeper, and one ball.

How to Do It: This drill teaches your player catching skills and eye contact. Have your goalkeeper lie on his or her back, head pointing towards you. Stand about four feet away and throw the ball to your goalkeeper to catch. They must watch the ball carefully to catch it.

Figure 13.53. Overhead Catch

Roll Ball (B)

What You Need: This drill uses you, your goalkeeper, and one ball.

How to Do It: This drill teaches your goalkeeper ball control and touch on the ball. Place the soccer ball on the ground and the cones in any order around the area. Your goalkeeper will move the ball with his or her hands through the course set up by the cones. Run this drill very fast so your goalkeeper can develop ball control and touch on the ball.

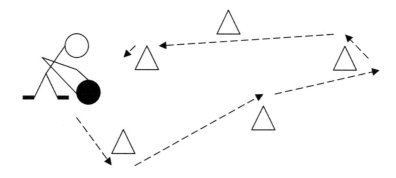

Figure 13.54. Roll Ball

Throw and Catch (B)

What You Need: This drill uses you, your goalkeeper, and one ball.

How to Do It: This drill teaches your goalkeeper concentration, quickness, and ball control. Have your goalkeeper stand with the soccer ball in hand, throw the ball into the air, go down on his or her knees, then jump back up and catch the ball before it hits the ground. They will have to move quickly to receive the ball. This is a good warm-up drill.

Figure 13.55. Throw and Catch

Catch a Throw or Kick (I)

What You Need: This drill uses you, your goalkeeper, and one ball.

How to Do It: This drill teaches your goalkeeper to play the proper position and develop ball handling skills. Set up the cones to represent the limits of the goal. Have your goalkeeper stand inside the goal area. You will move out and away from the goal and gently kick or throw the ball. By throwing from different positions on the field, your goalkeeper will be able to move to the ball and use the proper techniques. This is also a good time to have your goalkeeper return the ball to you. He or she can kick the ball (dropping it from the hands) or throw it to you. Make sure to work on the accuracy of kicks. Distance will develop as strength improves.

Throw or Kick

Figure 13.56. Catch a Throw or Kick

Punch the Ball (I)

What You Need: This drill uses you, your goalkeeper, and one ball.

How to Do It: This drill teaches your goalkeeper to punch the ball when he or she cannot catch it or control it. Punching the ball is used when the ball is high and needs to be redirected away from or over the goal. A two-handed punch is used when the ball is coming to the goalkeeper but the goalkeeper does not have room or time to catch it. In this case, he or she will use two hands to punch the ball back out onto the field.

Have your goalkeeper stand facing you. Throw the ball to him or her so it is above the head. The goalkeeper then jumps and punches the ball straight up. This causes the ball to continue its movement, but to deflect upward and over the goal. While still facing your goalkeeper, throw the ball and let him or her punch it with both hands to send it back toward the field.

One Hand Punch   Two Hand Punch

Figure 13.57. Punch the Ball

Collect the Ball (A)

What You Need: This drill uses you, your goalkeeper, and one ball.

How to Do It: This drill teaches your player actual goalkeeping moves and techniques. Set up the cones to represent the limits of the goal. Then place cones in front of the goal to represent defensive players. Have your goalkeeper stand inside the goal area. You will move out and away from the goal, and dribbling around, you will shoot the ball on goal. By shooting from different positions on the field, your player will be able to move to the ball and use the proper techniques. He or she will also have to maneuver around the defenders (cones). Have your goalkeeper return the ball by kicking (dropping it from the hands) or throwing it to you. They can kick the ball, dropping it from their hands like a football punter, or throw it to you. Make sure to work on accuracy. Distance will develop as strength improves.

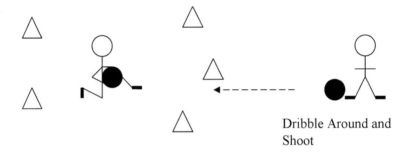

Dribble Around and Shoot

Figure 13.58. Collect the Ball

14

Start-and-Restart Practice

KICKOFF

A kickoff is used to start the game, to restart the game after a break for the quarter or half, and after a goal is scored.

U-6 Kickoff

For U-6, the best way to practice the kickoff is to place half of your team on offense and the other half on defense. Select one player to be in the center circle to kick the ball. Place the other offensive players to the right and left of this person and about ten feet away.

Have your defensive players stand on their side of the field, each directly in front of one of the offensive players.

The player kicking off the ball needs to kick the ball over the center line and to either the right or left side of the field. As soon as the ball is kicked, the offensive player closest to where the kickoff goes needs to move directly to the ball, receive it, and start dribbling toward the goal.

The player who kicked the ball off and the other offensive players need to move straight down the field. Do not let them run to the ball. This establishes the kickoff and also establishes positional play.

On defense, when the ball is kicked, the player closest to the ball moves to intercept it, and if unable to intercept it, tries to gain possession. Since most players will move with the ball, there will be more players from the offense than the defense around the ball. Teach your players that when they get possession of the ball they need to quickly kick the ball out into the open field where other players from their team can get the ball and have a free run on goal.

Switch the players around so they have the opportunity to play both offense and defense. This practice enables your players to learn the kickoff formation in addition to receiving, dribbling, and passing/shooting skills.

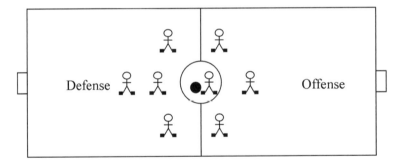

Figure 14.1. U-6 Kickoff

U-8 Kickoff

In U-8 play, kicking the ball downfield will not work. It will only give the other team the ball. When kicking off, place four of your players on the center line. Two will be inside the center circle and two outside the center circle. The two outside the center circle will be out on the wing, or edge, of the field.

Two players will be halfway between the center line and the goalkeeper. Have one of the players in the center circle roll the ball across the center line. The other player in the center circle will run to the ball and kick it back to one of the two players behind them at kickoff. The two players on the outside of the field will then run into the defensive half of the field.

The player that received the kickoff can dribble until challenged and then pass the ball down the field to a teammate who has moved across the center line. This gives your team control of the ball, and allows your players to move into the other team's defense, setting up a possible scoring opportunity.

Use your extra players as the defenders. Remember to switch the players around so all of them can play both offense and defense.

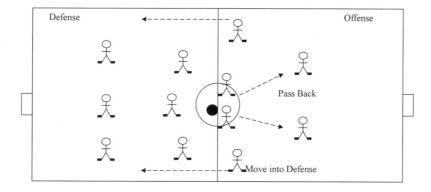

Figure 14.2. U-8 Kickoff

GOAL KICK

A goal kick is taken when the ball travels over the end/goal line and goes out of play and was last touched by the offensive team. To clarify, the offensive team in this instance is the team trying to score in the goal on that end of the field.

A goal kick is taken the same way for U-6 and U-8 players. The only difference is the strength of the kick and the number of players waiting to receive the ball.

The soccer ball will be placed in the corner of the goal box on the side of the goal where the ball went out of bounds. It is then kicked back into play by one of the defensive players. All goal kicks at this level should be kicked to the side of the field. It is important that your players not kick the ball straight out from the goal, because if they do, the ball can be easily returned into the goal for a score.

Post a player or players at the side of the penalty box and have the person kicking the ball kick it to them. It is possible the U-6 fields will not be marked with a goal box or a penalty box, however.

If on defense, put a player directly in front of the goal so if the ball is kicked straight out the player can return it to the goal. Have the other players on your team stay close to the offensive players.

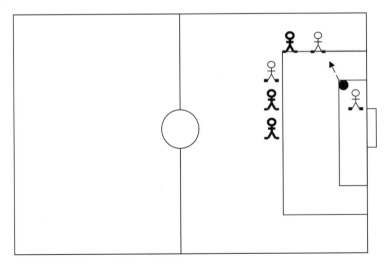

Figure 14.3. U-6 Goal Kick

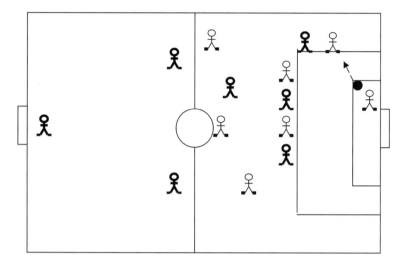

Figure 14.4. U-8 Goal Kick

CORNER KICK

A corner kick is used when the ball goes out of play over the end line and was last touched by the team defending the goal.

The corner kick is taken by placing the ball in the quarter circle in the corner on the same side where the ball went out of play.

Again, the procedure for a corner kick is the same for U-6 and U-8. The difference is the strength of the kick and where the players are posted on the field. Since the kicks for U-6 will not go far, a player will have to be within kicking distance of the player taking the kick to receive it, and another player must be positioned in front of the goal to kick the ball in when it is relayed to them from that player.

U-8 players have the strength to get the ball to the goal on a corner kick. This requires a player to be positioned between the kicker and the goal in case of a bad kick, and a player even with the front post and the back post of the goal. If by chance the ball is kicked beyond the goal, the person at the back post can easily go after it.

The object is to get the ball into the goal area so your team can score. If your team is on defense you will need a person between the kicker and the goal, one at the front post of the goal, and other players in the goal box. When the ball comes in, tell your defenders to clear it away and out of danger. It is again best to kick the ball to the side of the field so it is harder to return, but the most important thing is to get it out of your goal area.

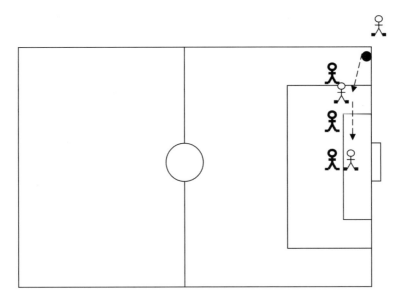

Figure 14.5. U-6 Corner Kick

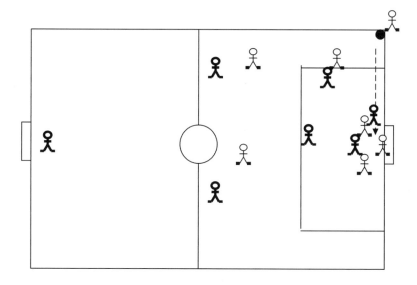

Figure 14.6. U-8 Corner Kick

INDIRECT KICK

An indirect kick is the result of a foul that is considered non-dangerous. The kick is placed at the spot of the foul and has to take an indirect path to the goal. This means the ball must be touched by another player before going into the goal. A shot directly into the goal that is not touched by another player will not count. If, after the first touch the ball is touched by another player on either team, the ball can be shot on goal and count.

For U-6 teams, just put a player to the left and right of the player taking the indirect kick. You can call out to the kicker where you want them to kick the ball. You can say, "Kick the ball to Heather or Billy." When that player receives the ball, they can either shoot on goal, if close enough, or dribble and then shoot. If the other team is taking the kick, just position your players near the other team's players. This provides the opportunity to gain possession of the ball. Remember your players have to be away from the person kicking to allow the other team to play the ball.

U-8 players can actually set up a formation that allows them to increase the possibility of scoring. The best way to do this is to make sure you have players that move into a position where they have an unobstructed view of the goal. The best defense is to ensure that none of the kicking team's players are open, and that the goal area is blocked.

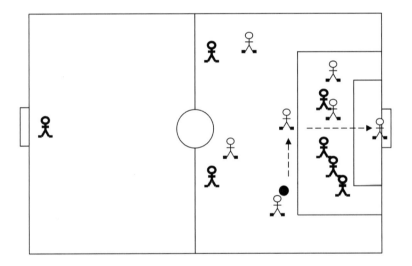

Figure 14.7. U-8 Indirect Kick

DIRECT KICK

Direct kicks are a result of a major or dangerous foul. This type of kick is not used for U-6 teams and is also not used for some U-8 teams. The defense for a direct kick is the same as an indirect kick, but the offense is different. If the player taking the direct kick has an open shot on goal, they should shoot directly at the goal. If the goal is blocked by the defense, he or she should use the same method as with the indirect kick.

DROP BALL

A drop ball is a technique used when the ball goes off the field after being touched simultaneously by two players, or when the game is stopped at a time when neither team has advantage or control of the ball.

A drop ball is accomplished with two players, one from each team, facing each other. The referee then drops the ball straight down between the two players. When the ball touches the ground the players are permitted to kick the ball. The drop ball is a method employed to restart the game without giving an unfair advantage to either team.

You can practice this by pairing your players and having them face each other approximately two feet apart. Drop the ball straight down between them. Remind the players they cannot kick the ball until it touches the ground. To do this they must watch the ball carefully. This is an activity where players (and referees) often get kicked, so be prepared.

PENALTY KICK

A penalty kick is not used for U-6. The kick is a result of a major foul by the defense that occurred within their penalty area. This is considered a direct kick and the referee places the ball on a designated spot directly in front of the goal.

The spot is marked on the field and is usually located about halfway between the goal and the edge of the penalty box. One player, from the team that was fouled, is picked to kick the ball. Normally the coach will select the player to take the kick.

The goalkeeper must stand on the end line, between the goal posts, and cannot move until the ball is kicked. All other players from both teams must stay outside the penalty box, and penalty arc, until the kick has been taken. In most leagues, the younger players do not take penalty kicks.

If the ball hits the goal posts or is blocked by the goalkeeper, the ball remains in play. If the ball goes outside the goal area (off the field) the game is restarted by a goal kick. If the ball goes into the goal, the action counts as a goal scored and the game is restarted with a kickoff.

15

Offense and Defense Drills

Scrimmages are very important to help the players to learn what they'll have to do in a game. Also, because it's fun for them, most young players will constantly ask you when they're going to scrimmage. The problem is that when your team is in a game or scrimmage, the players don't get very many touches on the ball and therefore scrimmaging isn't always an effective use of practice time.

There are drills that replicate the skills needed in the game that are fun and allow more individual contact with the ball. Scrimmaging is necessary to learn the different start and restart actions, but drills better prepare your players. Doing both will really aid your team's development.

Half Field Scrimmage
What You Need: Use of an area that is half the size of the normal playing field. One soccer ball, a goal or cones to replicate the goal, and your players split into two teams.

How to Do It: This scrimmage is identical to a real game except it is played on half of the field. Split your team into two halves, offense and defense. The offense will kick off just like in a game and move the ball down the field trying to score. All of the usual rules apply. If the ball goes over the end line or touchline it is brought back into play using the proper method of restart.

If the offense scores, they retain the ball and kick off again. If the defense is able to get the ball and dribble or clear the ball across the center line, then they become the offensive team and the teams change sides. If one team is dominating play, switch up your players to equalize the teams. The object of this drill is to perform a scrimmage but by limiting the size of the field allow greater results in less time.

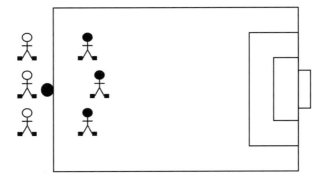

Figure 15.1. Half Field Scrimmage

Four Goals

What You Need: An area equivalent to approximately half of the normal playing field. You need one ball and eight cones to make four goals. Split your players into two teams.

How To: Set up the goals so there are two at each end. Place the players in the center between the two goals. You can either throw the ball into the field of play to start the drill or you can have one of the teams kick off. I prefer the ball being thrown in because it requires the players to move to the ball and try to capture it before the other team does.

A goal can be scored in any one of the four goals. For the 4- and 5-year-olds, they must dribble through the cones that form the goal to score. For 6-, 7-, and 8-year-olds, they must pass the ball through the cones and one of their own teammates must touch receive the pass for it to count as a goal. For the older players you can limit the number of touches on the ball to four, three, two, or even one touch. Using one touch is ideal for working passes. The object of this drill is for the players to learn to move to open area, pass, shoot, and dribble.

After a goal is scored, throw the ball up into the air again and let the players go after it to restart.

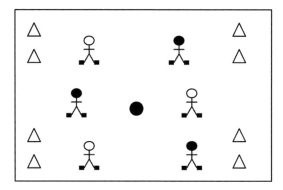

Figure 15.2. Four Goals

Dribble Control
What You Need: You need one ball, two teams, corner cones, and an area that is approximately half of your normal field size.

How to Do It: Place the cones in the corners to set the limits of the field. If you are playing on an actual field, the end, center, and touchlines become the borders. No goals are used in this drill. A player can score by dribbling to their end line or their center line and then stopping the ball on or beyond the line. I usually allow the players three steps to stop the ball.

The game is started by lining up one team on the end line and one on the center line. As soon as the ball is rolled onto the field the players may move to the ball. Emphasize proper spacing, keeping the players separated.

Scoring is accomplished by dribbling the ball to the line and stopping it or passing the ball to another player who is already standing on the line. If the ball goes out of play over the touch-line, the opposite team restarts with a throw-in. If the ball goes over the end line the opposite team starts with a kick from the end line.

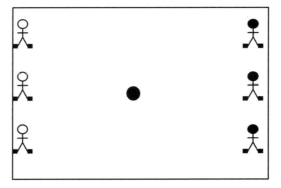

Figure 15.3. Dribble Control

Pass Control

What You Need: You need one ball, two teams, corner cones, and an area that is approximately half of your normal field size.

How to Do It: Place the cones in the corners to set the limits of the field. If you are playing on an actual field, the end, center, and touchlines become the borders. No goals are used in this drill. The object of this game is to see how many passes one team can string together before they lose possession of the ball to the other team. When the opposing team gains possession of the ball they then try to string together as many passes as they can to get the largest number.

This reinforces the need for the players to spread out and use the whole field for offensive passes. It also makes the team that is on defense spread out to cover all of the players. All balls that go out of play are restarted with a throw-in. The game is started by you rolling the ball into the field of play.

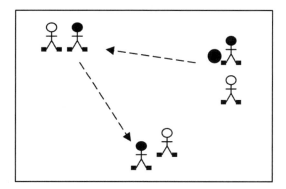

Figure 15.4. Pass Control

16
Game Preparation

PLAYER IDENTIFICATION

Remember, coaches do not play. They teach and observe their players. A U-6 team has three or four players on the field at a time and the normal formation is to have the players in line with each other. Multiple positions are not used.

If you have a U-8 team, and have six or more players on the field at one time, make out a listing that has four categories: goalkeeper, fullback, halfback, and forward. You do not have to match players to positions immediately. Observe your players and put their names under the category that you think they will be best able to play.

During the next practice of formation, put the players in these positions and observe them. Make changes as required. During the formation part of practice, you can put a full team together and use the other players in oppositional positions. Have the team wear the practice jerseys to help distinguish one team from the other.

I always liked to have the fullbacks, halfbacks, and forwards together, and they were my offense. They would do the kick off and then bring the ball down the field. You can observe their kickoff formation and playing formation. Make corrections as required. Then, on the opposing team I had the goalkeeper, fullbacks, and if I had enough players, I put in halfbacks. This team was the defense.

I was able to observe my players on both offense and defense this way. When you keep changing the players from one team to another you can see the different players in all situations, and they get to practice all aspects of the game. Keep updating your listing until you are satisfied with the players' positions. Once you are satisfied, put the players' names under the category you want them to play, and put the sheet on your clipboard.

Players Name	Goalkeeper	Fullback	Halfback	Forward

Figure 16.1. Player Positions

PRIOR TO THE GAME

Using a piece of paper, list all of the players' names down the left-hand side. Across the top put 1, 2, 3, and 4. Draw a line down the page between the numbers, and across the page before and after each name. You now have your game sheet.

Since many leagues are all-play, and there is a designated time each player must play, this will give you a schedule to ensure everyone plays and that you have the best possible team on the field. In the younger ages groups, U-12 and below, I always tried to play all of my players an equal amount of time each game.

Due to the number of players, some played more than others, but each played at least half of the game.

By playing everyone, they all improve. Some players will develop quickly while others will develop over time. Keep all of them playing, because that is why they show up for every practice.

Opponent:	First Quarter Start Time:	Second Quarter Start Time:	Third Quarter Start Time:	Fourth Quarter Start Time:
Name of Player				
Jones	FB		FB	
Smith		FB		FB
Allen	HB		HB	
Walker		HB		HB
Johnson	F		F	
James		F		F
Hollis		G		G
Williams	G		G	

Figure 16.2. Game Lineup

On your schedule, put in G (goalkeeper), FB (fullback), HB (halfback), and F (forward). Make sure each quarter is filled with a whole team that is balanced as best you can. Some players will invariably be weaker than others. If you have a weak halfback, put that player between a strong forward and a strong fullback for support. Balancing out your team enables you to be competitive all game long.

If you are playing a game with twenty-minute halves, get the second quarter players ready and standing by the touchline at the 9:30 mark on your stop watch. On the next stop of play, send the new players in. Since some games are not in quarters and you have to wait for a substitution time, you may have the new players in the game a little early or a little late, but the time will average out over the course of the season.

One of the first things you want to do is to get enough official game lineup cards from your league commissioner to cover all of the games throughout the year. Make these out after you have established the above playing schedule. By having the card ready prior to the game, you will not have to fill out the card when you get to the field and can give the game card to the referee early. When you get to the field, you need to be ready to start your team on their warm-ups and will not have sufficient time to fill out the lineup card.

Pre-Game Preparation

Set a routine that is comfortable for you for game preparation. Mine was very simple. When you arrive at the field, I suggest you:

- Set up your lawn chair even with the half line and five feet back.
- Pull out your stopwatch if playing halves and put it around your neck.

- Pull out the practice balls and line them up on the touch line, on the side of the field where you are going to have your team do their pre-game warm-ups.
- Sit down, relax, and have a cup of coffee, soda, or water and wait until your players arrive.

Once the players arrive, line them up in twos and have the team run a lap around the field. When they get back to the starting point (half line), have them turn and run to the center circle which they should position themselves around, facing toward the center mark. If the center circle is already taken by the opposing team, just move the players down the field a bit.

Lead your team through their stretches.

After the stretches, have the team form two lines, each even with the goal posts. Pass the ball to one player at a time and have that person take a shot on goal. If players miss the goal, they chase their own miss.

After two or three repetitions of this drill, have the team form three lines on the center line. Have the first player in each line advance down the field, passing the ball to the left, back to center, to the right, and then back to the center. This continues until one of the outside players is near the end line. As the player approaches the end line, he or she centers the ball and the other two move to receive it and attempt a shot on goal. Do this until each player has had two or three repetitions.

Take your players to your designated sideline and have each of them drink liquids and rest until game time. This is also the time you tell the players who is starting and who is going to be substituted in. After telling the players who is going in at what time, you never have to worry. You might get choked a couple of times as players come over and grab your stopwatch to see how much time has elapsed, and they will never let you forget the time.

Now is the time to turn in the game card to the referee.

With this done, it is game time. Sit down in the lawn chair and enjoy the game. Once the players are on the field, there is little you can do, except encourage your players.

GAME TIME

Do not coach from the sidelines. You can make minor corrections, such as "fullbacks move up," or "forwards, make more cuts," but other than that you can only encourage your players. Do not be the coach that runs up and down the sideline yelling at the players, because that does not help. The players need to learn how to play on their own, not wait to be told what to do. The time to make corrections is in practice or when the players are off the game field.

During the game, players will make mistakes. Make notes on these and address them in your next weeks' practice. Trust me, the players know when they've made a mistake. Let your players know everything is okay. Tell them "good try" or "that's the way to stay after the ball" or something else encouraging. Positive motivation goes a long way. Corrections are best made face-to-face with the player and on the practice field.

Many of the other coaches used to razz me about my "sit in the chair and drink my coffee" technique. But I always produced good players and winning teams. As commissioner of coaches, I encouraged this practice. I found this relaxing because I knew I had little, if any, control once the game started and the players were on the field. Sitting in the chair encourages the parents to sit back and watch, and it helps the players to relax.

Remember, this is the time to enjoy your hard work. You won't win every game, but if you see the mistakes and then correct those mistakes in practice, you'll win more than you lose.

POST GAME

Talk to the team after the game, but don't dwell on what went wrong. Focus your comments on what they did right. Keep the talk short, since most parents want to get home.

After you get home and relax for a while, write up what you need to practice the following week. This is your practice schedule. My wife and I would always stop and have coffee and discuss the game together. She is great at observing what players do correctly and incorrectly, and I relied upon her for suggestions. I also asked her to sit at the top of the bleachers, or if there were no bleachers, away from me so she could observe the game from a different viewpoint.

If she saw something amiss, she would let me know. Sometimes you need someone you can rely on to see the game from a different point of view.

17

Game Formations

The word formation refers to how the players are positioned on the field. Formations are designed to provide the ultimate offense and defense during play of the game. A proper formation allows the players to be evenly balanced throughout the field. Any arrangement of players on the field that provides balance is an acceptable formation.

There are common formations that are used and most coaches will go with a well-defined and proven one. However, sometimes you will see a special formation set up. Formations are designed to provide strong offense and defense with players of equal strength.

Formations are identified by starting with the fullbacks and moving through the halfbacks to the forwards (Example: 4-3-3.) The goalkeeper is not counted in these formation designators. If your team is playing with less than the standard 11 players, which is common for younger players, just decrease the numbers in each area while still maintaining balance throughout the field.

The U-6 rules vary by league and as such, so do the formations. Some teams have 3 or 4 players on the field with no goalkeeper, and some U-8 teams play with 6 or 7 players on the field, including a goalkeeper. U-8 normally plays with 6 players plus the goalkeeper for a total of 7. U-10 usually plays with 7 players plus a goalkeeper for a total of 8. The U-12, U-14, and older teams normally play with 11 players. Check your local league rules on player numbers.

We are going to start with a full eleven-player formation so you can see the symmetry used with a full team of players. Figure 17.1 is a 4-4-2 formation (4 fullbacks, 4 halfbacks, and 2 forwards) of 11 players that provides for both strong offense and defense. With this formation, the field is well balanced.

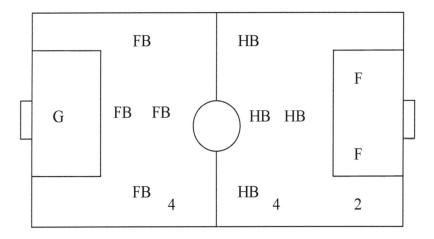

Figure 17.1. 4-4-2 Formation

The 4-3-3 formation, also an 11-player formation (Figure 17.2), is set up with four players in the fullback positions, three players in the halfback positions, and three players in the forward positions. With the 4-3-3 formation, the halfbacks can transition easily from offense to defense.

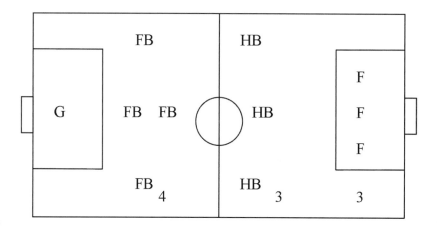

Figure 17.2. 4-3-3 Formation

The 3-2-1 (Figure 17.3) is a good formation for U-8 teams. This formation makes it easy for the players to keep their positions and provides good balance throughout the field. The U-6 and U-8 players have a tendency to play the ball rather than play a position, chasing after the ball rather than maintaining positional discipline.

The 3-2-2 (Figure 17.4) is another very good, balanced formation. Adding one player changes the formation to a 3-3-2 formation (Figure 17.5). If playing with nine players, the formation can also be changed to a 4-2-2 formation or a 3-3-2.

Most U-6 teams do not have a set formation, although as a coach you need to keep emphasizing to your players to maintain separation. Figure17.6 is an example of that separation.

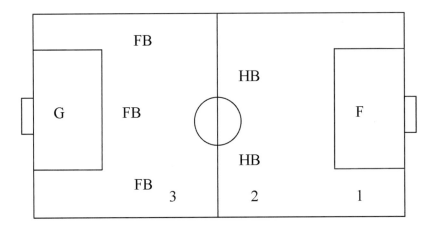

Figure 17.3. 3-2-1 Formation

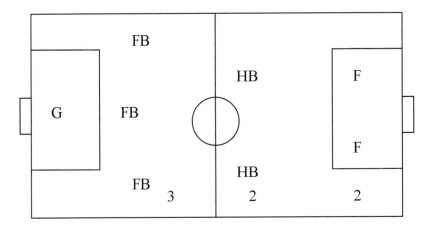

Figure 17.4. 3-2-2 Formation

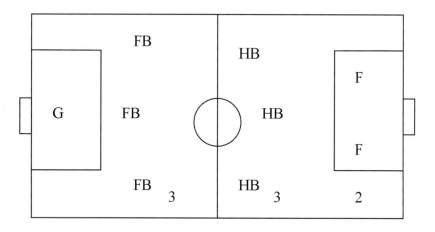

Figure 17.5. 3-3-2 Formation

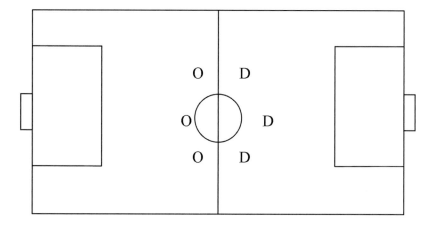

Figure 17.6. 3 Vs 3 Formation

18

Nutrition and Water

This is basic information that you should know about nutrition and water. The more you know the better it will be for your team. This will tell you what they can eat if you have an early game, if there is a short time before the game, or if there is a long time. Parents will ask you for this information.

SOURCES OF PROTEIN

Meat and nuts
- Builds muscle, rejuvenates injuries
- Long-term benefits for building muscle

CARBOHYDRATES

Sugar, pasta, potatoes
- Energy—main source of fuel
- Sugar is a simple carbohydrate, while starches are complex carbohydrates.
- Carbohydrates are converted into glucose and glycogen.

- Glucose is used in the blood to deliver immediate energy.
- For sustained energy, glycogen is stored in the liver.

FATS

Energy reserve
- Most potent source of energy

PRE-GAME MEALS

Always choose high-carbohydrate and low fat foods. This ensures easy digestion and fuel for energy.
- Top-up fluid levels. This leaves you comfortable, neither too full nor too hungry. Proper fluid levels leave you feeling confident and ready for action.
- Eating a high carbohydrate diet in the days before a match and drinking sports drinks during the match keeps players running faster and further in the second half.

Here are some of my recommendations, depending upon game time:

Three hours or more before the game:
- Pancakes, pasta, baked potatoes, juice
- Pizza, which consists of all elements of nutrition

Short time before the game:
- Bananas
- Tomatoes
- Peanut butter
- Sports drink

DRINKS

According to the Australian Institute of Sport, "Sweat losses of 1–2.5 liters [around 1–3 quarts] per 90-minute game in cool conditions and approximately 4 liters [around 1 gallon] during hot conditions have been reported in some studies. However, the reported fluid intake of players was typically less than half of the sweat rate."

Below are tips for better fluid intake during soccer:

- Drink sports drinks, which encourage better fluid intake because of their taste, as well as supplying extra fuel for the game.
- Drink well during warm up and half-time breaks.
- In hot weather, especially, be creative in finding ways to grab a drink during the play of the game. Some players leave their bottles around the side of the field and dash for a drink whenever there's a stoppage in play. I've seen other teams use small plastic bags of ice that are thrown to the players. Some parents or other players just hand ice to their teammates when there is a stop in the play
- Practice good drinking strategies in training sessions. Make sure you give plenty of water breaks to your players.

AVOID CAFFEINE

A word of advice: caffeine drinks (tea, coffee, etc.), raise blood pressure and cause the heart to beat faster. Caffeine serves to stimulate you or pick you up, but caffeine can also limit vitamin and mineral absorption, having a negative effect on energy. Caffeine drinks are not for the players, so leave them to yourself and the parents.

19

Knowing Your Players' Characteristics

Some people will try to tell you that younger players will not be able to play soccer and will look like a bunch of ants swarming around the ball. This is not true. They will do what they are trained to do, whether they understand it or not. For example, when I was coaching, a parent once approached me and asked if it was possible to serve as an assistant coach, since he wanted to coach his child's team and had played soccer but never coached. I was coaching U-12 at the time and agreed. I forgot to tell this new coach that the U-6 players would not be able to do what the U-12 players were doing.

He coached with me for three seasons and then started his own team. About four weeks into the season, he called and asked if I could come to see one of his games. I agreed and asked him how he was doing. He stated that his team had won every game, and the closest score was fifteen to one. I was astounded when I saw his team.

They had a proper kickoff formation, moved the ball to the outside of the field, moved down the field, centered the ball, and scored. Their throw-ins were to their own players. In other words, they were far advanced compared to the teams they were playing. They didn't understand the concepts, but they knew what to do because of training.

When you are working with your team, you will find out that younger children have different characteristics than older children. Because of these characteristics, the style you use must be altered to compensate and achieve the best results. Below are some of the characteristics that best describe young players in the U-6 and U-8 age groups:

• *Short attention span*
Unable to sit for lectures or anything that does not include them doing something to keep busy.

• *In their own world*
Their lives are themselves. They do not think of others nor do they work well as a team.

• *Feelings hurt easily*
Raising your voice or even saying something was done wrong can hurt their feelings. They need constant positive motivation to develop into good players. If you make them feel good about themselves they will do whatever you ask them to do.

• *Limited hand/foot-to-eye coordination*
Your players will see the ball coming toward them and they will kick at it, often missing the ball or kicking other players. This skill develops as they do more drills that require them to kick the ball.

• *Very limited catching skills*
Most players will not be able to catch the ball. The U-6 and some U-8 teams do not use a goalkeeper. Limited ability to catch the ball

is one reason, but the main reason is so all of the players can develop actual soccer skills. Since the only person that is required to catch the ball is the goalkeeper, this will not be a large problem.

• *Like to run and jump, no realization of pace*

They have constant motion and a high energy level. They love to run, jump, and play games, but they possess no pacing ability. They will continue at full speed until they are completely worn out.

• *Lack conceptual knowledge*

They have not developed concepts. They may not understand that each team has a goal. On one occasion I had a player score five goals in one game and we won three to two because my player scored twice in the wrong goal. The player knew to score, but the concept of different goals was not part of his understanding. As a coach, five goals scored by your team is great. Who cares where they were scored?

On another occasion, two teams were playing, one in red and the other in blue. A red team player broke toward the goal with the ball. This player's coach was yelling, "Wrong way, you are going the wrong way." But no fear, the other team, the blue team, was also well coached. When they saw the player break for the goal, they chased down the player and took away the ball before the player could score.

In each case, the players were doing what they were trained to do. Concepts are not developed at this age and are not important. Telling them they did a great job is. Also distances and locations are not developed. You can't say, "Go out about ten yards." The player may go three feet, or disappear over the horizon.

• *Will do what they are told*

Your players will do what they are told to do or trained to do. They will take you at your word literally. For example, I once told a player to go in at halfback. The player asked where that was. I pointed and said stand where that player is standing. I sent in the player and as the ball came down the field past him, there was no movement. After the ball had rolled past the player three times I called for the player to come over to the side, and asked why the player was just standing there. I was then told that I had said "stand there."

• *Decent balance*

Children will have decent balance, but better balance and agility will come with time, practice, and age.

20

Handling Parents and Other Situations

As a coach you will have situations arise that you have never had to face before. Most can be handled very easily, but others may require assistance. In all the years I coached soccer, I only encountered two situations in which I needed assistance to handle a problem parent. It may or may not ever happen to you. Even if it does, don't let them spoil the coaching experience for you. You could be the best person in the world and still run across individuals who will not like what you're doing. Just remember that the majority of the parents do appreciate your efforts and will support you in difficult times.

Don't let the situations listed in this chapter scare you or even worry you. They are here to give you an idea of what to do if the situation ever arises. Most of these will never happen, but if they do, you'll be ready.

Situation #1
You establish the playing positions and a parent is not happy with where his or her child is playing.

This is a common complaint that is easy to handle. If you are comfortable with where you placed the player, let the parent know that you put the player there because you feel they can be a real asset to the team in that position. Let them know that if it doesn't work out, you will move the player to a different position. Go with your instincts, as you are less biased than a parent.

If you agree with the parent and want to change the player's position, let them know that in the next game you will move them and see how the player performs in the new position.

Situation #2

A parent is not pleased because someone on the team is getting more playing time than his or her child.

Since practically all soccer organizations require that each player play at least half of each game, this normally isn't a problem. There are times, however, when you will have players miss games and you will have to play others a little more. The natural instinct is to play your best players to give your team an edge. You can do this, but I always found that if I used multiple players, they all benefited from increased playing time.

Situation #3

You hear that parents are unhappy because your child plays more than the other players on the team.

Some coaches have the attitude that since they are spending their time coaching, that gives them the right to play their own child more than the others. Other coaches tend to think that their child is a better player than the others and should be played more. Don't get caught up in this mentality. Your child is only one of the members of the team and shouldn't be treated any differently than the others. The other side of the coin is that it's hard at times, when you see your child making mistakes, not to over-correct.

By playing your child more, or by being overly critical, you are separating him or her from the team. Your child and other players and parents will see this, even if you don't. I have seen many good players quit because they were either expected to be the star player or were constantly told about their mistakes.

Situation #4

You have a referee who consistently calls your games poorly.

Not every referee will call a perfect game. If you have a referee who doesn't seem to understand the rules, or has other problems, call the head referee and ask to have someone observe this referee. It may be because the referee is new, or it may be that he or she is officiating in an age group that is above his or her capabilities.

An example is this: I had a referee that had called many of my games over the years, but with my older players the referee always seemed to be out of position. I called in and reported this and the referee was observed and was transferred to officiate for the younger players. The referee was very good, but was unable to move at the speed necessary in games in which the players were older.

Situation #5

You have a child who is constantly late to practices or games, or misses them completely.

Get the player's parents off to the side and ask them if there is a problem. If it's a transportation problem, get with the team manager and see if alternate arrangements can be made with another parent. Sometimes it's just that the family is disorganized and is late for everything. If that's the case, let them know how important it is to have their child at the field on time and hope for the best.

Situation #6

You have a player who starts crying and either sits down or walks off the field.

With the younger players, this will happen to you more than once. It is usually because someone else got the ball or because they were bumped or kicked. If they are really hurt, take them off the field and take care of them. If it's just their feelings that are hurt, let them know that they won't get the ball every time and that getting bumped or kicked happens and that the other player didn't do it on purpose.

If the player wants to leave the field, let them and then let their parents take care of them. Let the parents and the child know that when they are ready to go back in to let you know. If you don't hear anything for a few minutes turn and ask the child if they are ready to go back in and play. If they are, send them in. If not, let them stay where they are. In time, they will outgrow this kind of behavior.

Situation #7

You have a player who just stands on the field and doesn't take part in the game.

Over the years I have given labels to certain types of players. There is the artist, the player who draws pictures in the dirt. There is the pilot, the one who watches airplanes overhead, and the bird watcher, who watches the birds in the sky. You may have the train engineer, the player who stops to watch a train. You also may have the flower picker, the player who picks grass, clovers, or wildflowers from on or near the field.

Again, relax, as this behavior will change with time. Younger players have a short attention span and are easily distracted. Enjoy the wonders of youth.

Situation #8

You have a player who isn't interested in playing soccer and is afraid of the ball.

Most young children are playing because their parents want them to play. The child may not want to play. The best you can do is to try and get these players actively involved in every drill or activity. Let them know that the closer they are to the ball the less chance they have of getting hurt. When they are close to the ball, it will normally hit below the knees and will bang against their shin guards. If they are at a distance, the ball can hit them above the waist.

One season I picked up some new players and one of the parents approached me and told me that his child didn't like soccer and was afraid of the ball. He stated that his child just wanted to stay in the house and read or play computer games, and they wanted him to get some exercise. He went on to say that he didn't care if his child got much playing time. He just wanted him to do something that was physical.

First of all, we were in an all-play age group where every child had to play half of the game. Second, even when I had teams in higher divisions without that rule, I still tried to play everyone at least half of the game. The players don't come to every practice and work so they can sit on the bench. I also found out that when I had missing players, or was in tournaments where we had multiple games over a short period of time, I could shuttle in the players without a loss of proficiency.

The parent was correct. The player didn't want to play soccer and tried his best to stand off to the side. I didn't let that happen. I got the player involved in every activity and most times selected this player as the captain for drills. Although it was a slow process, the player started to get involved and by the end of the season was playing good soccer.

This method doesn't always work, and you may have to talk to the player and find out what other activities they are interested in. One of my players wanted to play tennis and the parents got the child on a tennis team. Years later I read in the paper that this child had received a college scholarship for tennis. Not every child is best suited for soccer.

Situation #9
You have a parent who is verbally abusive to his or her own child or others on the team.

The best way to handle this is to ask the parent not to yell at the players. This doesn't always work. In one situation I asked a parent to refrain from yelling at the players, but he ignored me. On the next stoppage of play, I asked the referee to please remove the person from the playing field. The referee was glad to do this and when she talked to the person she gave him two options: he could leave on his own, or she would call the police. He left on his own and never came to another soccer game. A few weeks later his wife approached me and thanked me. She said that for the first time, she and her child were enjoying the games.

Situation #10
You have parents who threaten you

You have two ways you can respond to this situation. One, you can try to calm them down, which seldom works, or two, you can turn and walk away. I suggest the latter because if the parents are so out of control that they are threatening you, they are not going to listen to anything you have to say to them.

This actually happened to me and I walked away and then called the organization's president and informed him. I then filled out a letter of complaint against both parents and asked that they be banned from the practice field and the playing field. I also asked to keep their child on my team.

The parents were mad because they felt that the other players were picking on their child and accused me of letting it happen. In reality, at every practice I had to stop *their* child from picking on *other* players, but their child was just a normal eleven-year-old. He was a little hyper, but still a good kid. I didn't want the player to miss out on playing with his friends. The child played with my team the remainder of the season and the parents watched from the parking lot, behind the fence.

Situation #11
Do you coach boys and girls differently?

The simple answer is yes and no. There are a few differences you need to be aware of whether you are coaching a boys team, a girls team, or a team with both boys and girls.

Teaching the actual skills doesn't differ. Strength is less of a factor in soccer than in many other sports. Kicking the ball a long distance isn't a major factor in soccer. Kicking the ball with accuracy and proficiency is important, and that can be done equally well by boys and girls.

So what is the difference? It comes down to the attitudes of the children. Whether we want to believe it or not, boys and girls are raised to have different values. If a coach yells at young girls, they may cry, yet boys may just get mad and act out. Girls will stop and think about what they are told by the coach, analyzing what is being said. Often boys will just go do it.

If you feel that girls can't be as good at soccer as boys are, don't try to coach girls. If you do, you're going to fail. You might also want to go watch some ladies teams in high school and above. But I need to caution you—prepare to have your mind changed.

Coaching styles can impact your players. Sometimes you have to be direct and commanding, other times understanding and warm. Boys and girls need both. Don't coddle your girl players. If one of your players gets hurt, treat her like you would a boy. Some coaches use a misguided concept of the fairer sex to protect their female players. Don't do this. Treat the boys and girls equally.

Just remember, there are differences between boys and girls, but they learn the same skills, and play the same game. The girls usually insist on fair play, while boys may not care and may want only to win. All you have to do to be a successful coach of either boys or girls teams is to understand there are some differences in attitudes, but not in playing skills and drills.

> You may have a situation arise that you are not sure how to handle. If that happens, call your age group commissioner, director of coaches, director of referees, or whoever you think can help. You have a whole organization behind you just waiting to help you. Don't hesitate to talk to others.

21

Fun Things to Do

Making soccer fun for you and your team is a must. Also, the more involved you can get the parents, the easier everything will be for you. There are things that you and your team's parents can do to make the whole soccer experience more fun for everyone.

BUILD A TUNNEL

When the game ends, the players from both teams will go back out onto the field, line up on the center line facing each other, and then move forward to give "high fives," shake hands, or just say congratulations.

When your team comes off the field is when the parents get involved. A fun way is to have them build a tunnel for the players to run through.

This can be done by the parents lining up on the center line, starting at the touchline. Have them face each other, one across from the other, with space for the players to run between the parents and underneath their arms.

Have the parents raise their arms and place the palms of each hand against the parent's hands across from them. This makes an archway or tunnel for the players to run through when they return to the sideline.

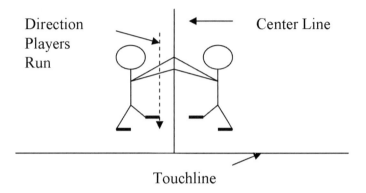

Direction
Players
Run

Center Line

Touchline

Figure 21.1. Building a Tunnel

The younger players love this and the tunnel is also fun for the parents. Forming the tunnel gets everyone involved and honors the players. The outcome of the game is not the point. The point is to let your team and the others know that everyone is proud of them.

TEAM SIGN

Many teams have small signs that they put up behind the coach or at the side of the bleachers. These are signs that identify who the team is and often the names of the players on the team. Spending a lot on money putting together a sign is not necessary. Most teams change at least some of the players every year and often change their team names or colors.

The sign should be big enough so it can be seen across the field, but not so large that it is hard to handle. A three-by-four-foot sign is a good size, although you may want to go four-by-five foot. Don't go any bigger.

If you have someone on the team that sews or is handy at crafts, he or she will be able to do the sign very easily. All of the parents can chip in on the cost. If the labor is free, the cost will be minimal.

There are numerous ways to make the sign. One is to get a piece of cloth that is thick enough to sew a border and the players names on. The flag or the border can be the color of the team.

Let's say the colors of the team are orange and white. The background can be white and the border, player names, and team name or logo can be in orange. They can all be sewn on the background.

I prefer the name of the team only, with the logo. This can be used year after year. If the names are put on, use Velcro attached to the names of the players. That way the names can be changed as the players change.

Another way to do this is to just get heavy felt, get lettering from a craft store, and then glue on the letters. Again, you don't want to get too elaborate, just something that identifies the players and that the players can look at with pride. The sign or banner can have hooks on all four corners or can be put on two poles so it will stand on its own.

If your team normally plays where there are bleachers, then the clips can be used to fasten the sign to the top of the bleachers. Get creative, but keep this inexpensive.

Try to get this finished before the first game of the season.

PARENTS VS. PLAYERS GAME (PICNIC)

Talk to the parents and set up a team picnic day at the end of the season. The event needs to be held at a soccer field, and the highlight of the day will be the soccer game with the parents against the kids.

Remember, this is for fun. The parents should not try to be professional players. Let the kids be the superstars of the day. Tell the parents to hold back on the strength of their kicks and to limit their challenges. Remember, the parents are a lot bigger and you don't want the kids to get hurt. Also, make the game short, as the players will have a lot more energy than their parents will.

Part of the picnic can involve handing out the team's pictures, if they were taken, and any trophies the team won that season. Some teams purchase small trophies or medals for each player regardless of their actual game results.

If the parents and players are going to give the coach a thank-you plaque, this is the time they can present it to you. Remember, this is a day dedicated to the players and you, the coach, for all the hard work throughout the season. This is also a great way to just have some family fun.

The whole family can attend the picnic. Grandparents, aunts, uncles, cousins, friends, etc., and you can encourage the families to bring their video or still cameras. This will make for years of fun memories.

PROFESSIONAL SOCCER GAMES

If you have a professional soccer team in your area, it is great to gather up the players and parents and go to a game. Let the players wear their uniforms.

Many of the players will spend more time eating nachos, popcorn, sodas, and hot dogs than they will watching the game, but they will still enjoy the experience. Most coaches who take the team for the first time mistakenly think that the team will learn by watching the professional team play. They may pick up a little, but generally speaking, they will just have a lot of fun.

Major League Soccer is obviously the best; however, with that being said, any level of professional or semi-professional soccer will suffice.

If none of those are available, college soccer is also great. Most areas also have high school soccer and again, these games can be a lot of fun. The idea is to go as a family and team and have an enjoyable time at the game.

TOURNAMENTS

Talk to the league officials and other coaches and ask about taking your team to soccer tournaments. Most tournaments guarantee all teams play at least three games. The idea is not to win everything and end up world champions, but to gain experience playing teams from other areas and to have fun.

Most areas have local tournaments, so you don't have to travel and stay in motels or hotels. These tournaments are a lot of fun and the more games the team plays, the better they will get.

A side benefit is that most tournaments sell T-shirts with the tournament name and logo. The kids and many parents like to get these to wear. I have never gone to a tournament that my team did not enjoy. Tournaments are harder on the parents than the players, but then again, most things are.

SOCCER CLINICS

Soccer clinics have become standard. They are normally one week long and concentrate on teaching the basic skills of the game. Many college soccer coaches put on clinics and use their players to help teach them. There are also many clinics taught by companies and leagues. These are also great.

Most clinics are taught in the summer and the players will learn more about soccer, make new friends, and come away with T-shirts and balls from the camp. Check out the different camps in your area, as some will be better than others. Decide which is best for the players on your team.

FUND-RAISERS

Finally, to keep the costs to a minimum, the team can hold fund-raisers to generate money. This is something the parents and the players can both get involved in.

A car wash is easy to do and can bring in good money. Dress the players in their uniforms, but make sure they wear old shoes. Many service stations and other businesses will let you set up on their property and use their water for free. Don't be afraid to ask. Look for a location close to a corner where there is a lot of traffic passing by.

Parents can bring wash mitts, sponges, buckets, soap, and other items used to wash a car. Cardboard signs can be made for the kids to hold up to get customers. A card table can be set up to collect the money. If you keep the price low, you will attract more customers.

If you ask for a donation, many people will not come because they are not sure what to pay. Don't go over four hours, usually 8 AM to noon, or 10 AM to 2 PM, are the best times to catch people out running their errands and shopping.

Don't forget, the parents will do most of the work. The players will get wet and have fun, but they normally don't wash a lot of cars.

Another way to raise funds is to have a bake sale. Parents can bake cookies, cakes, brownies, etc. Most high traffic stores will allow the teams to set up a table near the entrance(s) to raise funds for their teams. Pick out a store that has high walk-in volume and then check with the manager of the store in advance.

There are other ways to raise funds for the team, but don't make fund-raising a hassle. Keep it simple.

Remember, soccer or any other sport can be a family affair if you get everyone involved. Creating and maintaining that involvement will make the season more fun for you, your team, and the parents.

Glossary

advantage clause: A soccer rule that gives the referee the right to have a team or player continue play after a foul is committed by the opposing team. The foul is not called if calling the foul would take the advantage away from the player or team in possession of the ball.

age: This is used to determine which age group a child will participate in. It is a date set to ensure all children are near the same age. It is usually set for the end of July or first of August.

alignment: How the players are positioned on the field, normally associated with a playing formation. Alignment must provide balance throughout the field.

arc: This term is most frequently used to describe the "penalty box arc," which is the arc at the top of the penalty box. It can also refer to the quarter circle, which is sometimes called the "corner arc."

arc of concentration: An area extending from each goalpost through the corner of each goal box and each penalty box, going out to the separate touchlines. This is the area in which most goals are scored. The defense must try to keep the ball out of this area.

assist: This action is a pass that precedes the scoring of a goal. A player makes a pass that assists a player who scores.

assistant referees (linesmen): Two people who assist the on-field referee by controlling the touchline and watching for offsides infractions. Each assistant referee has a flag that is raised when an infraction occurs.

attack: An attempt to score while having possession of the ball. This can be made by a player or a team. It occurs when the team has the ball and is on offense. It doesn't matter where the ball is on the field. If the team is moving the ball to score, it is an attack.

attacker: A player on the team that has possession of the ball.

B

back: Defensive player that plays nearest the goal. These players are often referred to as fullbacks, or left, right, or center backs.

back pass: This is a term meaning to pass the ball backward instead of forward.

back post: The goal post that is located the farthest away from the player with the ball. This is also referred to as the "far post."

back side: The side of the goal opposite from where the ball is being played.

ball: The soccer ball comes in three sizes: 3, 4, and 5. The size of the ball used is dependent upon the age of the players.

banana kick: Kicking the ball into the air and making it curve like a banana. The curve is created because of sidespin on the ball. This type of kick is also referred to as "bending the ball."

balance: Balance is how the team addresses the other team's players. In other words, how they play in relation to the person with the ball.

beat: Getting past a player.

bicycle kick: A specialty kick often referred to as a scissor kick. This kick is accomplished by advanced players. A bicycle kick is executed by falling backwards while bringing one's feet into the air, causing the player to have both feet off the ground. The kick is made by bringing the feet forward, over the head, and striking the ball with the foot while the player is upside down and in the air.

blind side: The area behind a player.

boot: This word has two meanings in soccer. It means to kick the ball, and is also another name for a soccer shoe.

boundary lines: Marked lines on a soccer field that indicate the outer perimeter of the playing area. The boundary lines are a maximum of fives inches wide.

box: Term used most commonly for the penalty box area of the field. Sometimes the term is used to indicate the goal box area.

breakaway: When a player gets past the defense and moves on the goal undefended, creating a one-on-one situation with the goalkeeper.

bylaws: The rules and regulations used by the soccer leagues to establish local policy.

C

caps: An old term derived from swapping hats at the end of an international game. It now refers to the number of official international games a player has played in for his or her national team.

card: A card that is pulled from the referee's pocket and shown to indicate a serious infraction of the rules. Two colors of cards are used: red and yellow. A red card removes a player from the field and the game, and a yellow card is a warning that further infractions will result in expulsion from the game.

carry: Another name for dribble.

caution: The act of showing a yellow card by the referee.

center: To center the ball means to kick the ball from the side of the field to the center of the field. This is normally a tactic used while in the vicinity of the opponent's goal. This gets the ball into the arc of concentration, which increases the chance of scoring.

center circle: The area in the center of the field used for starting play. The ball is placed in this area at the beginning of the game, and the beginning of the second half. The center circle is also used to start play after a team scores. The opposing team cannot enter the center circle until the team kicking off has played the ball. The maximum size of the center circle is ten yards in radius.

center spot: A mark to indicate the center of the center circle. This is where the ball is placed for kickoffs to start or restart play.

challenge: A term used to indicate when a defender tries to steal the ball from an offensive player.

charge: An act of rushing a player and hitting the other player by using one's body. This is a foul.

chest trap: When the ball is received on the chest and falls to the player's feet so that the player can play the ball.

chip: When the ball is kicked into the air as a pass or shot. This is kicked just hard enough to go over the head of the opponent.

clear: To clear the ball means to get the ball and remove it from a danger area as quickly as possible.

coach: The person in charge of training the players and conducting the players during their games.

cone: A plastic device with a larger bottom than top used as an aid during practice to mark specific areas. Often it is a bright color like safety orange.

contain: A method used to limit or restrict the opponent's ability to move or advance.

corner arc: A quarter-circle marking that is on each corner of the field. The ball must be placed in this area to restart play after the ball is kicked over the end line by the defending team.

corner flag: A flag mounted on a pole placed on the exact corner of the field. This flag enables the players to see the maximum boundary of the field's four corners from a distance. The flag should be a minimum of five feet tall.

corner kick: The method used to restart play after the ball has crossed over the end line, going out of play, and was last touched by the defensive team (team guarding the goal). The offensive team puts the ball into play by kicking it out from the corner arc.

counter-attack: A term to indicate that your team has gained possession of the ball by a turnover and has stopped the attack of the opposing team. This is the start of their own attack, which "counters" the other team's attack.

cover: A defensive term that means to stay close to your opponent.

creating space: A term meaning to move away from your opponents to make it easier to pass or dribble the ball.

cross: To send the ball from the outside of the field directly in front of the goal. It can also mean to move the ball from one side of the field to the opposite side.

cross bar: The top post of the goal.

D

danger zone: The area directly in front of the goal often referred to as the arc of concentration. This is the area where most goals are scored.

dangerous play: Any action taken by a player that can result in injury to another player.

defense: The actions required to protect the goal and prevent the opposing team from scoring.

defender: The players with the primary role of defending the goal.

deflection: When the ball hits and bounces off of another player or goalpost.

deliver the ball: Making a good pass to a teammate.

depart: When a player leaves the field of play. Players are not allowed to enter or depart the field without official referee permission.

depth: The placement of players on the field. Good depth is when the players are evenly dispersed from end-to-end across the field.

depth of field: The length of the field from one end line to the other end line.

direct kick: The type of kick used after a major foul has been committed. On a direct kick, the ball can be kicked directly into the goal and count as a goal scored. Direct kicks are indicated by the referee pointing his or her arm directly toward the goal.

distribute: Used to indicate a goalkeeper's kick. Goalkeepers distribute the ball to a specific player or players on the field.

draw: A game that ends with a tie score.

dribble: Moving the soccer ball by using one's feet. Proper dribbling allows the player to maintain control of the ball.

drills: The activities used during practice to teach players how to further develop their skills in soccer.

drop ball: A technique use by the referee to restart the game. This is done by dropping the ball between two opposing players. Neither player can kick the ball until it has touched the ground.

drop-kick: A term to indicate a type of kick that can be used by the goalkeeper, who will drop the ball and kick it after it bounces back up.

E

encroachment: A term used to indicate that a defender is too close to the offensive player on a start and restart. A predetermined distance must be given to allow the ball to be put back into play.

end line: The boundary line at each end of the field. This is also referred to as the goal line where it crosses inside the limits of the goal.

enter: A player can only enter the field during a restart and with the permission of the referee.

equipment: The items used by the coach or player to practice or play the game of soccer.

F

far post: The goal post that is farthest away from the player. This post is commonly referred to as the back post.

fast break: Advancing the ball past the defense and toward the goal before the defense can respond.

feint: Making a fake move to beat a defensive player.

field: The area marked on which teams play the game of soccer. Fields vary in size depending upon availability of land. Small-sized games are played on fields of reduced size.

field player: The team players on the game field, excluding the goalkeeper.

field the ball: A term meaning to play the ball or to put the ball into play.

FIFA: Fédération Internationale de Football Association. This is the international governing agency for soccer.

finish: The act of ending a play by scoring in the opponent's goal.

flank: The outside of the field (wing) closest to the touchline.

flick: A term used to mean that a player is relaying the ball or moving it on to another player without stopping the ball. This can be done by a head or foot pass.

foul: Any infraction of the rules.

foot trap: A technique used to stop the ball using your foot.

formation: A formation is a term used to indicate the placement of the players on the field. Formations are always indicated by the count starting with the fullbacks. The goalkeeper is not included in the count and the count can never exceed a maximum of 10. A 4-4-2 formation is the number to indicate 4 fullbacks, 4 mid fielders, and 2 forwards for a total of 10.

forward: This is the name of a player who has the primary duty of scoring. They are the players located closest to the opponent's goal.

forward pass: Passing the ball so it moves down the field toward the opponent's goal.

free kick: Any kick awarded to a team as the result of an infraction of the rules.

futbol: The official name of the game of soccer. It is commonly used in every country except the United States and Canada.

G

game clock: The official elapsed time that remains in the game is the game time. The official time is kept on the field by the referee.

give and go: This is a pass where the player passes the ball and then moves to a position to again accept the ball. This is sometimes called a wall pass.

goal: The goal is the rectangular area at each end of the field that has a maximum width of eight yards, a maximum depth of six yards, and a maximum height of eight feet. The front edge of the goal is directly on the end line. The back of the goal is covered by a net to stop or catch the ball after the ball has entered the goal.

goal scored: When the ball travels into the boundaries of the goal and is completely over the goal line, this is a score. Each goal scored counts as one point.

goal box: The small marked rectangular area that is located directly in front of the goal. The goal box is a maximum of twenty yards wide and six yards deep.

goalkeeper (goalie, keeper): The goalkeeper is the player who works directly in front of the goal. When the goalkeeper stops the ball the stop is called a save. The goalkeeper can only use his or her hands while inside the penalty area. No other players on the team can use their hands while on the field of play. Goalkeeper's are required to wear a different color jersey to distinguish them from the other players on the field.

goal kick: One of the methods used to restart play after the ball has traveled over the end line and was last touched by the offensive team. The defensive team places the ball in the goal box and kicks the ball out to restart play.

goal line: This is the portion of the end line located between the goal posts.

goal post: The vertical poles on the goal.

goal side: A term used to indicate the placement of a defensive player between the offensive player and the goal.

H

half: The game is split into two equal halves of time. The halves are divided by a period called halftime.

halfback: The halfback is a player positioned in the formation between the fullbacks and the forwards. They are also referred to as midfielders.

half line: The line marked on the field that divides the field into two equal halves. The center circle is on this line.

halftime: The period of time between the first half and second half of the game. This period is used to allow the players to receive instructions, rest, and drink liquids.

half volley: This is a type of kick that is performed by allowing the ball to bounce on the ground and then be kicked while in the air.

hand ball: This is an infraction of the rules caused by a player touching the ball with the hands or arms while on the field of play.

hat trick: Three goals scored in one game by a single player.

header: A skill where a player uses his or her head to pass the ball or shoot on the goal.

holding: The act of grabbing another player by the body or clothing to stop that player from moving freely.

home team: The home team is the team that normally plays on the field the game is being played on. In the case of league play where all teams play on the same field, a team is designated as the home team. The home team normally furnishes the ball and linesmen if needed.

I

in bound: Throwing the ball into the field of play.

in bounds: When the ball remains inside the boundaries of the field.

in play: When the ball is being played while inside the boundaries of the field.

indirect kick: A type of kick used to restart play after a minor foul has been committed. The ball must take an indirect route to the goal. To do this the ball must be touched by another player after the original kick before going into the goal.

injury: When a player is hurt while on the field of play, the play will continue until the referee blows the whistle.

injury time: When a player is hurt while on the field of play, the referee will stop the game and the game clock. Injury time is added to the end of the game or half. This is at the discretion of the referee.

instep: The portion of the foot from which the soccer ball is normally kicked. This can be on the inside of the foot or on the laces of the shoe.

J

jersey: The shirt worn on the field by a soccer player. Each team will wear shirts that are different colors. The goalkeeper is required to wear a shirt that is distinctively different than those worn by the other players on the field.

juggling: The act of bouncing and controlling the ball using the feet, thighs, and head. The ball is moved from one part of the body to the other while maintaining control.

K

keeper: A short, slang name used for the goalkeeper.

kick: Striking and moving the ball using the foot.

kickball: A term used to indicate players running all over the field and kicking the ball rather than playing soccer.

kickoff: The method used to start a game or restart play after a goal is scored.

knock off the ball: A technique used by defensive players to move the opponent away from the ball. This is done by having the players keep their arm straight along their side and using pressure to move the offensive player off the ball. Sticking out elbows and arms or shoving players is an infraction of the rules.

L

laces: Refers to the instep of the foot, which is where the laces of the shoe are located.

laws: The rules of the game that govern the play and conduct of the soccer players.

leading pass: A kicked or passed ball that ends up in front of another teammate. This type of pass allows that player to move to the ball without changing speed or direction.

linesman: The two people that assist the referee by controlling the touchline and looking for offside infractions. These people are also called assistant referees.

long ball: A ball kicked by an offensive player that ends up traveling beyond the group of defensive players on the field. This allows a teammate to move to the ball unopposed.

M

major foul: Any infraction of the rules that is dangerous to players on the field.

manager: The person that assists the team coach by making telephone calls, arranging rides for players, and performing other tasks that allow the coach to concentrate on the training of the players.

mark: A term used to indicate a player that is placed in a position where he or she play one-on-one with an opposing player.

match: The name for the actual soccer game.

minor foul: An infraction of the rules, but an infraction that is not considered a dangerous play by the referee.

midfielder: A player who is located on the field in a position between the fullbacks and the forwards. They are also referred to as halfbacks.

N

near post: The goalpost that is the closest to the player with the ball.

net: The type of covering used on the back and sides of the goal. This is a net that can be seen through, but which stops the ball when the ball enters the goal.

nutmeg: The act of kicking the ball between the legs of an opposing player.

O

obstruction: When a player uses his or her body to play or interfere with another player rather than playing the ball. This is an infraction of the rules.

offense: Moving the ball toward the opposing goal with the objective of scoring.

official: The referee and linesmen, or assistant referees. These are the only officials that have responsibility for controlling and governing the game.

offsides: A rule that is intended to keep an offensive player from standing in front of the goal of the opposing team. Offensive players must have one defender between them and the goal-keeper when the ball is kicked to them by their teammates.

one touch: A pass or shot of the ball by a player only touching the ball one time. This is done by shooting or passing without dribbling.

open space: This is a term used when a player moves to an area on the field where there are no other players.

opponent: The team you are playing.

out of play: A term used to indicate when the soccer ball or a person is outside the boundaries of the playing field.

overlap: The act of running past another of your own team-mates to advance down the field and get in position for a pass or shot.

own goal: This is the name for the goal your team is defending. It is also the term that describes the act of scoring in one's own goal.

P

pace: The speed of the ball or player. It is also used to indicate the speed of the game.

pass: Moving the soccer ball from one player to another using feet, head, or other part of the body (with the exception of the hands and arms).

penalty arc: A portion of a circle located on the outside center of the penalty area. This area is not part of the penalty area, but is an area players must stay outside to maintain a specified distance from the ball during a penalty kick.

penalty area: The rectangular area directly in front of the goal that serves as the boundary within which the goalkeeper is able to touch the soccer ball using his or her hands.

penalty kick: The free kick used to restart play when a major foul has been committed inside the penalty area by the team defending the goal. The restart is accomplished by placing the ball on the penalty mark. One player from the team fouled enters the penalty area to take the kick. Only the goalkeeper from the defending team and the person kicking the ball are allowed inside the penalty area.

penalty mark: A mark placed on the field inside of the penalty area. This mark is where the ball is placed for a free kick after a direct foul has been committed inside the penalty area.

pitch: A term used to denote the soccer playing field. It is a term that is used for most sport fields in the United Kingdom.

play on: A term used by the referee to inform players to continue play. This is normally heard as a result of the implementation of the advantage rule.

player: A member of a team engaged in the game of soccer.

point: The unit used to denote a goal scored. There is one point counted per each goal scored.

possession: This is a term that indicates your team has control of the ball.

power shot: A hard shot that is normally taken on goal in an attempt to score.

practice: The activity used to teach and condition the players to learn the game of soccer.

pressure: Keeping close contact with a player to keep them from advancing or scoring.

Q

quarter circle: The marking used on each corner of the field. The ball is placed in this area to restart play after the ball is kicked over the end line by the defending team.

R

rainbow kick: A specialty type of kick that is accomplished by putting the ball between the feet, using one foot to roll the ball up the back of the leg, and using the heel of the other foot to kick the ball over the players head from behind. The ball travels from the rear of the player to the front, taking the arc made by a rainbow.

rebound: When the ball hits the goalpost or another player and bounces back into the field of play.

receiving: The act of gathering or collecting the ball.

recover: When a team loses the ball and the players are caught out of position. The players must get back into the proper position.

red card: A red-colored card about the size of a playing card used by the referee to inform a player and team that the player is being ejected from the game. This player cannot be replaced by the team and the team must therefore play one player short.

redirect: Changing the direction of a moving ball by using a pass or a kick.

referee: The official on the field that is responsible for enforcing the laws of the game.

restart: A term used to indicate when the ball is put back into play after a stoppage of the game.

rules and regulations: The laws and amended laws used by the soccer leagues to establish local policy.

run: The move made by a player, with or without the ball, to get into another position.

S

save: A term used to indicate that the goalkeeper stopped the ball from going into the goal.

score: The points earned by each team. Each goal counts as one point.

scrimmage: When a team plays another team in a practice game.

settle: The act of controlling the ball.

shield: Protecting the ball from an opposing team player. This is done when the player places his or her body between the opposing player and the ball.

shin guards: A protective device worn under the socks to protect the player when they are kicked in the shins.

shirt: The jersey worn by soccer players.

shoes: The footwear worn by soccer players. Soccer shoes are designed to give the player traction and allow the player to kick and dribble without the toe of the shoe snagging on the ground. There is no cleat underneath the toe of the shoe. The cleats are dispersed throughout the sole.

shoulder charge: A legal play that allows a defender to press against the person with the ball to move them off the ball.

shorts: The short pants worn by soccer players. The color of the shorts can either match or contrast with the jerseys worn by the players.

shot: When the soccer ball is kicked, headed, or passed toward the goal by a member of the offensive team.

shoot out: An action that is used when the game ends with a tied score. Each team will get five kicks from the penalty spot, using different players that are one-on-one with the goalkeeper.

short: A term meaning to play with fewer players than allowed.

skills: The psychomotor actions a player is required to learn to properly perform the techniques in the game of soccer.

slide tackle: A move where one player slides or moves into the ball to take or knock the ball away from the opponent.

small-sided: A term used to indicate the number of players on the field. It is used to indicate play when there are fewer than the standard eleven players.

socks: Garments that cover the feet and the shin guards on the players. Socks are required to be knee high. These can match or contrast with the uniform.

square: Positioning of a player when he or she is directly to the right or left of the player with the ball.

start: This term is used to denote the beginning of the game at the first and second half.

steal: To remove or take the soccer ball away from an opponent.

stoppage time: The time added onto the game for any stoppages. These can be the result of an injury, a ball out of play, a substitution, or other events deemed as a loss of playing time by the referee.

stopper: The defender that plays in the front of the other defenders and is positioned closest to the center line.

strategy: The approach used by the coach to formulate the game plan.

striker: The center forward on the offense.

strong side: The side of the field the ball is on.

substitution: The act of replacing one player on the field with another player who is off the field. This can only be done during certain restarts in the game and with referee approval.

support: When a player or players move into a position to assist and support the player with the ball.

sweeper: The name used to identify the last defender who plays in front of the goalkeeper.

T

tackle: The name of the action used by players when they slide into the ball to take or knock it away from their opponent.

techniques: The actions generated by skills that enable a player to understand and participate in the game.

throw-in: The method used to restart the game after the ball has traveled out of bounds over the touchline. The ball is thrown in by the team that did not cause the ball to go off the field.

time out: Though not an official term used in soccer, this word indicates the stopping of the game clock, which is kept by the referee.

through pass: The act of passing the soccer ball so the ball goes beyond the defense to a teammate in open space. This is a pass used to give an offensive player the ball as he or she moves behind a defensive player.

toe kick: An improper kick used in soccer. This is used to denote the ball being struck by the toe of the shoe. It is an inaccurate type of kick.

touchline: The line that marks each side of the field. This is the boundary for the width of the field. This line is also referred to as the sideline.

trap: Stopping the ball to gain control. This action can be performed with many different parts of the body.

tripping: Causing someone to stumble or fall. This is a major infraction of the rules.

turnover: Losing the ball while the game is in play and having possession change over to the other team.

U

under: Sometimes identified as "U." Used in the game of soccer to denote the age of the players. Under is used in conjunction with a number. U-8 means the players must be under the age of 8.

uniform: The shirt, shorts, and socks worn by team players.

V

victory: Winning the game.

vision: The ability of a player to see openings and other players while on the field of play.

volley: Kicking the ball while it is traveling through the air.

W

wall: The positioning of players, side by side, to form a line to prevent a kick from going through to the goal.

wall pass: A technique using two or more players to pass the ball around an opponent. This technique is also called the give-and-go.

width: Layout of players from side to side on the field. Good width is even spacing covering from touchline to touchline.

width of field: The area from one side of the field to the other.

wing: The outside area of the field which is closest to the touchline.

winger: A name normally denoting a forward who plays on the right- and left-hand side of the field. The term is sometimes used to describe any outside player.

winning: Scoring more points than the opposing team.

World Cup: Soccer games played every four years by professional teams from all participating and qualifying countries in the world. This is the largest sports event in the world and is controlled by FIFA.

Y

yellow card: A colored card about the size of a playing card that is used by the referee to warn a player and team that the player is being cautioned for an infraction of the rules.

Z

zone play: When players are situated in a set area of the field that they must defend.

Acknowledgments

For most published authors, writing the book is the easiest aspect of the process. The hardest and most extensive part is the publication process. For me it has been made simple and enjoyable. This is due to three main people and their staffs.

My agents, Chamein Canton and Eric Smith, from the Canton-Smith Literary Agency, stepped forward and ran with the ball. They are truly a dream team. The other person is Mark Weinstein, senior editor at Skyhorse Publishing. Mark was the first editor willing to take a chance on a new author who lacked commercial writing credentials. His previous actions kickstarted my writing career. It is a real pleasure to be working with him again.

No book would have been possible without my best friend, partner, and wife, Mary. She is my in-house editor, sense of reasoning, and most avid fan and critic. If I can get a book past her I know it will be well received by others.

I would also like to thank my children, Denise, Jay, and Tony, and my grandchildren, Bobby and Rylyn, who have provided many hours of enjoyment while I coached them and watched them play the game of soccer and other sports. My son Jay is one of the beginning coaches who took the time to review this book.

To everyone who has been a part of this book, thank you.

About the Author

Robert "Bob" Koger grew up in Columbus, Kansas and now calls Holliday, Texas his home. Prior to becoming a writer, Bob spent twenty years in the U. S. Air Force, two years as a technical writer for a fortune 500 company, and eighteen years working for the Department of the Air Force as a civil servant.

Bob joined the Air Force after graduating from high school and became an aircraft navigation equipment technician. From there he went into teaching other Air Force personnel. He also spent four years as a military training instructor, or drill instructor. During his time in the Air Force he traveled all over the United States and also to a few exotic vacation spots such as Thailand and Vietnam.

Upon his retirement from the military he started his next job as the lead technical writer for Keuffel & Esser Company, where he wrote repair and operational books on laser ranging devices, heart monitors, and many other types of equipment made by the company. After about 2½ years the company decided to move their operations to New Jersey; and, wanting to stay in Texas, Bob resigned and went back to work for the Air Force in a civil service capacity, as an education and training specialist. For the next eighteen years, he worked in numerous faculty and staff positions before becoming the dean at one of the major Community College of the Air Force campuses.

During his time with the Air Force, Bob received two Associate of Applied Science degrees from the Community College of the Air Force, and received his Bachelor Degree from South West Texas State University, now Texas State University.

After retiring from civil service, Bob took off a few months to just work around the house and catch up on some fishing. Early in 2003, he started writing and after finishing his first book, he signed with the Canton-Smith Literary Agency. Shortly thereafter he signed a contract with McGraw Hill Trade to publish his first book, *101 Great Youth Soccer Drills*. The book was released in April of 2005.

Besides writing books, Bob also writes a weekly opinion column for Texas newspapers. His "As I See It" pieces cover a wide spectrum of issues. Among some of his favorites hobbies are: fishing, reading, swimming, and growing roses. He enjoys spending time with his best friend, who also happens to be his wife Mary, and his family. He has a daughter, two sons, a grandson and a granddaughter.

Bob spent over twenty five years coaching youth soccer. He has his United States Soccer Association "D" level Coaching License, and has coached all levels of youth soccer, including

Olympic Development. Bob has coached in Texas, California, and Mississippi. He also taught a coaching development clinic he designed. His teams have played teams from all over the U.S. as well as from Mexico, England, and Germany.